*charlie*
MUSKRAT

Library and Archives Canada Cataloguing in Publication

Johnson, Harold, 1957-
Charlie Muskrat / Harold Johnson.

ISBN 978-1-897235-44-7

I. Title.
PS8569.O328C43 2008   C813'.6   C2008-900084-6


Cover and book design by Jackie Forrie
Printed and bound in Canada


Thistledown Press Ltd.
633 Main Street
Saskatoon, Saskatchewan, S7H 0J8
www.thistledownpress.com

Canada Council    Conseil des Arts                    Canadian    Patrimoine
for the Arts      du Canada                           Heritage    canadien

We acknowledge the support of the Canada Council for the Arts, the Saskatchewan
Arts Board, and the Government of Canada through the Book Publishing
Industry Development Program for our publishing program.

# *charlie*
# MUSKRAT

## HAROLD JOHNSON

*thistledown press*

*charlie*
MUSKRAT

THELMA SCARES THE SHIT OUT OF me. It is not that she never talks to me or that when she looks at me her face indicates her extreme disgust. My wife's big sister is two years younger than Lois. Thelma weighs over four hundred pounds and no one dares call her fatty. That woman does not have an ounce of fat on her body. Not that I have ever seen her body. I just know. I know because when she carries in firewood, she carries nearly a quarter of a cord at a time. When she splits wood, stand back. If her half-ton goes in the ditch she drags it out, pushes it back straight on the road, then bends the springs when she squeezes back behind the steering wheel.

This story is not about Thelma, but it all started when Lori told me that Thelma was coming to visit again. It was not that Thelma was coming to visit that starts this story but that we were low on meat. The Moose I shot last fall was not going to be enough to feed that woman. Lilla wanted me to go shoot another Moose.

"It's the middle of winter." I tried to find a way out.

"Morris gets Moose all winter. Ask him how he does it."

I was stuck. Morris did get Moose in winter. He gave most of it away. Maybe I could get out of hunting yet, maybe Morris would donate a hindquarter to help feed Thelma.

"I'm out." Morris turned his palms upwards. "Why are you asking? You're as good a hunter as I am."

"Deep snow, cold, walk for days out there and not see anything."

"Do like I do. I just drive along the road, when I see a Moose I shoot through the window of the truck. Just don't get excited and forget to open it first."

So I did. I went road hunting. It was a little embarrassing, driving down the road with my rifle on the seat beside me, a thermos of coffee and a bag of Cheezies. I really hoped my ancestors were not watching but I knew they were. I felt their disapproval. At least I was alone. No one would be telling stories about me.

Lisa did not have to know how I got the Moose. She wouldn't ask. But I would have to tell the story of the kill, the hunter's story. How the tricky Moose tried to outsmart me or how he gave himself in sacrifice. Maybe I could leave out the part about the truck. Lolla would not ask for details. She didn't want to hear the story more than once anyway and I think she only tolerates the stories because it's tradition.

Lotte likes tradition. It has grown on her. My best excuse for whatever I need to get away with is to blame it on tradition. It goes back to when we met. Alcatraz. We occupied the famous island prison and no one cared. We didn't even get a headline "Indians Take Back the Rock". I don't remember why I was in California in the first place. It was that time. Wine was fifty cents a gallon if we drove inland and the old van made it there and back to the beach. Somebody had an idea, a radical idea. We all wanted to be radical back then. So we joined the occupation.

I was far from home, no one would know. I would not embarrass my family. Those were my freedom thoughts back then.

As soon as I stepped off the boat onto the rock someone recognized me. "Charlie Muskrat! What the hell are you doing here?"

Imagine that. I was thousands of miles away from home and whom do I meet, someone from my hometown. And my hometown was only a couple of hundred people up at the North end of Montreal Lake, Saskatchewan. Not that there was a hometown left either. The government moved the town across the lake and renamed it Weyakwin. All that was left in the old town were the mounds of dirt and collapsed cellar holes where the houses once stood.

As it happens, when people from the same place meet far from home they hang out with each other. That's what happened. Mary and I just started hanging out together and we never stopped. The only thing I wish that had happened differently is that I wish that I had not tried to be hard to get. Mary was not trying to get me. I remember that much but not much more.

"I'm going to have trouble remembering your name. It doesn't mean anything other than that I have a poor memory for names." I told her. And damned if after that show-off statement that meant that I had so many women in my life that I could not keep them straight, I've had trouble remembering Lorna's name ever since.

I don't rightly remember how we got from Alcatraz back home. It took a while. Montana was in there somewhere. I remember that much. I don't remember when Louise became my girlfriend or even when she started calling herself my wife or when I started calling her my wife. Shame of shame I do not remember when we first made love or when I first brought her flowers. She does. She remembers exact years dates and even the time. Teases me with it. "Remember the first time we made love?"

"Uh huh."

"Tell me again what you told me that morning."

"Don't you remember?"

"I remember, I just want to hear it again."

Then I'm stuck. And she laughs and hugs me and kisses my forehead like I'm a little boy and walks around with a big smile all bright again.

I remember some things. Important things. Like when we stood on the shore of the lake and looked at the overgrown old place. "I want to live here," she said. Just like that. And I said, "Okay," and started pacing off an area to build our house. That's how it's been. I don't know how many years we've been together. But they've all been like that. For a long time I think we were just friends. We came and went and came and went and were always happiest when we were together. We did not decide to live together. We just did. It was either she did not go home or I did not go home or we both went home together. There must have been a time when we were boyfriend and girlfriend but I don't remember when it started or when it ended.

"Do you remember the first time you told me you loved me?"

"Uh huh."

"Tell me again what you said that afternoon."

"Don't you remember?"

"I remember, I just want to hear it again."

Laughs, hugs, kisses and smiles.

I do remember that we never had a ceremony, that we never made a commitment, that we are not married in white man law or in Indian law. I think we started calling each other husband and wife after other people started calling us that. "It's okay sir, your wife already paid for the gas." Now we have been together for so long that we know what each other is thinking. Like the other night when I was skinning a muskrat with a dull knife and Flora brought me the sharpening stone I was wishing I had handy.

We never talked about leaving it all behind and living away. There was no discussion about luxury or the lack of luxury. We just moved into the house we built together, ate from the garden we planted. I trap and hunt and get along and she works sometimes when we need money but mostly we don't need money and we just get along.

Wanda and I have never had a fight. Not once have we ever argued. Not that I remember anyway. She wants to do something and I help. She says we need wood and I get the axe. She says we need water and I walk down to the lake with the buckets. She says we need meat and I go hunting.

I think we are getting old now. My youngest brother just turned forty. The baby of the family is forty. He grew to be the biggest of us all and keeps reminding us that he is over six feet tall and weighs more than two-hundred pounds. We say that is because when we were young we had to get off the teat when the next baby came along. He got to nurse until he was in grade eight. Even so, we are all getting older. All of us except Wilma. She still looks as good as always. More importantly she acts like she's twenty-one. Keeps me laughing.

But I am getting older. I know because things hurt now. Joints and muscles and things like that. I can still walk twenty miles in a day checking traps and such. But the next day it's hard to get out of bed. Harriet makes the fire on those mornings and puts extra cinnamon in the oatmeal and lots of raisins. What's really strange about having greying hair is that younger people ask me for my opinion. I know enough to know that I don't know a hell of a lot. I usually answer by telling the asker a story. That's strange too. I remember stories.

Well, this story is about what happened when I went road hunting. I didn't have much of a chance to actually hunt. No sooner had I set out on what was to become an adventure, I picked up a hitchhiker. The old gravel highway that runs down the East side of Montreal Lake occasionally has hitchhikers. Trappers and such on their way to La Ronge for supplies, that sort of thing. I know all of these people and am used to providing rides, passing on messages or taking a list and a few dollars with me to pick up something someone ran out of.

He was standing on the side of the road. I tucked my rifle under the seat and pulled over.

Today's hitchhiker was a stranger. I asked the usual questions. "Where you going? What's your name? Who are you related to?"

"Down the road a ways. My name is, uh, Wesley, yeah, Wesley Jack, Wesley Jack that's my name. Who am I related to? Well let me see. Do you know . . . um . . . um." He scratched at the mat of tangled grey hair that showed from under his toque. "Well I guess I'm related to just about everyone."

No need to push things I figured. Anyone who was unsure of his name must have a reason to be vague. "Well, that's where I'm going too. Just down the road a ways." I didn't have to tell him I was road hunting. Maybe I was just going for a ride. Maybe I was just going to check my Rabbit snares, down the road a ways.

"What's your mom's name, Charlie?" Wesley Jack asked.

"Her name was Roberta. Roberta Muskrat. Her mom was Rose and her grandma was Catherine." There, I had told enough history and genealogy to place me properly in this world. I belonged here on this highway. My family had been in this area for many generations. But I did not remember telling Wesley my name was Charlie.

I tried humour. Best way to make a friend I always found was with laughter. Make someone laugh and their defences go down. Something about laughing, it's always easier to do when it is shared. I tried gentle teasing.

"Wesley Jack. Are you related to Whiskey Jack, Black Jack or Wesakicak?"

It worked. Wesley cackled loud and long, turned a long tooth smile at me. "Can't put nothing over on you, Charlie." And cackled some more. I laughed too. It was easy to laugh with this man. Suddenly, my anxieties were gone. I felt new. Wesley felt like a relative, one that I had not seen in a long, long time.

"So Charlie, I always wanted to know. How's your dad?"

"Oh, I haven't heard from him in a long time. Went back South years ago. I don't even know if he's still alive or not." I answered all relaxed and easy. So relaxed that I wanted a smoke. I offered one to Wesley. He took it. Sniffed the tobacco end, and sincerely said "thank you."

That was an odd thing to do, almost ceremonial, but everyone has their own reaction to tobacco. I offered coffee from the thermos, apologized for not having water. I did not have food either. I offered some of the left over Cheezies from the half empty bag. Wesley drank the coffee, commented upon its excellent flavour. "Dark Roast," I explained. "Perked on a wood stove."

"This is good Charlie." Wesley washed down the dry Cheezies with the coffee. "How you doing for gas?" he asked as he leaned over and tapped on the gas gauge.

"About half a tank, little better maybe. It should get me where I'm going."

"Yeah, it should." Wesley agreed. "I think I'll get out about here."

Here was nowhere. Nobody lived near here. This was just an old gravel road and muskeg on both sides for the next couple of miles. A good place to expect to see Moose in the summer.

"Are you sure?"

"This is a good spot."

"Hope I didn't insult you with that Whiskey Jack comment."

"Naw, that was good. You did good, Charlie. Don't worry about a thing. I'll see you again sometime."

This seemed strange, but who am I to tell someone where to get off. I figured I'd just keep hunting and I'd probably see him again when I came back this way with a Moose in the back of the truck.

Snow bent the trees along the road, arched them over away from the thick of the forest. The road was hard pack. The best part of winter driving, no mud or ruts. Thunder cruised along, his tires sung with the crunch of packed snow.


WESAKICAK'S MOCCASINS FLOPPED ON THE MARBLE steps all the way up Mount Olympus. The cool smooth stone felt kinda nice where the soles of his feet touched it through the holes in his moccasins. He was tired when he reached the top. Wesakicak felt his age. **It was a long time since the** beginning of the world. He refused to fly since 9/11, and it had been a tough paddle across the big pond to this far away place. The canoe trip reminded him of when Muskrat swam down in the water for land and the making of Turtle Island. That was a long time ago. Now there was this Charlie Muskrat thing to take care of.

He sat on the top step and leaned against a white smooth pillar. It wasn't as comfortable as leaning against a tree, but it supported his aching back. A man with a single long black braid down his back stopped on his way out and looked down at Wesakicak. He just stood there and looked, so Wesakicak asked "Who are you?"

"I'm Adonis." He pulled in his sagging stomach, rolled his shoulders back and pushed out his chest. "I'm one of the Greek gods."

"But, you're Chinese."

"I am not Chinese. I am Asiatic, according to the poets."

"I thought I was in the Greek Heaven."

"This is Mount Olympus, home of the great Zeus and all of his descendants."

"Who are you?" Wesakicak realized he had already asked that question, so he decided to ask it a different way. "Who are you related to?"

"I am Adonis. My father is my grandfather. My mother was Myrrha, but now she is a tree."

"Weird" Wesakicak thought.

"Barbarians are not allowed here." Adonis seemed unsure what else to say to Wesakicak.

"I had nothing to do with Barbara Ann. That must have been my cousin Nanabush. Us Cree don't fool around with white women."

"Oh, here is Hermes. Hermes would you escort this barbarian off the mountain?"

"How come you got sea gulls in your shoes and in your hat?" Wesakicak asked Hermes.

"Those are not sea gulls. I am the messenger of Zeus and I have winged shoes and a winged hat. What are you doing here?"

"Who are you related to?" asked Wesakicak.

"Who wants to know?" The wings on his hat fluttered like a seagull defending a scrap of garbage on the beach.

"Me."

"Who's Me?"

"I thought you were Hermes, the guy who walks on seagulls"

"I am Hermes, and those are not seagulls. I am the god of travellers and thieves."

"Thieves?" asked Wesakicak.

"Yes, thieves. I was born at dawn and by noon I had stolen fifty head of cattle."

"You're a rustler."

"I am a messenger for Zeus." The wings folded back, stiffly.

"I thought you people hung rustlers. Almighty Voice was cannoned to death for killing his own cow."

"I know nothing about that. What is it you want here?"

"Oh yeah, you guys have the right to remain silent, I'd forgot that."

"I know nothing about that either."

"What do you know?"

"I know that when mortals die, I escort them to the house of Hades."

"Is that your, how do they say in the movies, your happy hunting grounds?" Now Wesakicak was now getting somewhere.

"I know nothing about the hunting. It is told that there is a Plain of Asphodel but it is not written whether they hunt there. All I know for certain is that I take a Shade to the ferryman, Charon, and he takes them across the river Styx if they can pay the fare."

"Pay the fare? You mean with good deeds and valour and things like that?"

"No, they must pay the ferryman with money. They need a coin, an Obolos to cross."

"Hmm, that might not work. Charlie usually doesn't have any money."

"Who is Charlie?"

"I thought he might be one of yours. His father was Greek and his mother was Cree. She thought he said he was Creek. You know like the Indians in the States. But anyway, now we have Charlie and we don't know what to do with him."

"If he is a barbarian he cannot go to the house of Hades in any event. Perchance he is a Christian and can go to the Gates of Pearl and there state his case to Peter. There are many who follow the Christian road these days. In fact very few mortals seek the house of Hades anymore."

"Christian you say. I never would've thought of that." Wesakicak looked out across the world from Mount Olympus. It was a good world, blue and green, white puffy clouds drifted lazily, easily across the sky. He thought about it. "Maybe Charlie was a Christian." He thought about it some more, closed his eyes and tried to imagine it.

Hermes and Adonis looked at each other, then again at Wesakicak. "Is he asleep?" Adonis asked.

"I know nothing." Hermes answered.

"Hey, barbarian." Adonis nudged Wesakicak with his toe. "You have to move along now. You cannot sleep here."

Wesakicak opened his eyes, looked up at the two men in white dresses staring down at him. "I wasn't asleep." He lied. "I could just about imagine Charlie as a Christian."

"You will have to imagine it somewhere else." Adonis pulled in his stomach again.

"It's okay, my friends." Wesakicak leaned forward from the pillar. "I can see that Charlie would not like it here." He pushed himself to his feet. "I'll go check with him, see if he might wanna go somewhere else." He started down the long steps.


I PAID ATTENTION TO THE SOUND of Thunder's engine, the sound of his tires on the hard pack snow and the occasional bit of gravel exposed by the grader. It sounded good, everything purring and humming. Thunder would tell me if anything was wrong, if a spark plug was fouling or a tire was going flat. I didn't need vehicle trouble. I needed a Moose. There was a promising dark spot up the road that turned out to be another hitchhiker. I tucked the rifle back under the seat. It wasn't seeing much daylight today.

"Harold Johnson, what the hell you doing out here?" I asked my old friend.

"Damn snow machine threw a track. I had to leave it out there in the muskeg."

"You need help to go get it?"

"Naw, it's just a couple of bolts rattled loose. I'll go home and strip them off my brother's tractor. I've stolen so many bolts off that tractor this winter that I'm afraid when we fire it up next spring it's going to fall apart. I'll be all right. Have to walk back out here tomorrow and fix it. It seems I've done a lot more walking since I bought that machine than before."

"That's the way it goes." I agreed. "So how you making out? Any luck hunting this winter?"

"Not bad. I got lucky trapping. A few Otter. The price of fur sure is the shits, though."

"Yeah," I agreed "it sure is. What about Moose?"

"Tracks, that's all I've seen. Lots of Wolves around. They make a big loop from my place up to the Bow River and across toward Thunder Mountain. After they come through the Moose and Caribou are gone."

We rode along for a while. Harold was glad for the coffee I offered. Then I asked. "How's the writing coming along?" I was hoping for a Moose hunting story.

He looked at me as though I had said something I shouldn't have.

"I'm working on something."

"Tell me."

"Well, it's kinda just in the development stages. Don't worry, you'll get to see it before anyone else. I promise."

"Give me another story, then. Any Moose hunting stories?" I really wanted a Moose.

"Funny you should ask. As I was walking out I thought up another Wesakicak story. I'll try it out on you to see how it sounds."

I poured a coffee, lit a smoke and let Thunder slow down a bit. I was in the mood for a good story.

"First I have to apologize to Wesakicak for making up stories about him." Harold looked toward the roof of the truck as he began. "Kayas." He started in tradition. "Well, it seems that Wesakicak got lice. Big ones. Anyway, Wesakicak was a good hunter back then." I gave Harold a quizzical look. Everyone knew that Wesakicak was a poor hunter. Oh well, it was Harold's story. He could tell it anyway he liked. "He had a wife and a couple of children and was a good provider, brought back meat all the time," Harold continued. "His wife was a good woman, generous. She was proud that Wesakicak was a good hunter and she liked to go around the camp and give meat away when Wesakicak killed something. Well, this one time Wesakicak brought home a Moose. She cooked for him and after he ate he went to sleep. When he woke up he wanted something to eat. But she had given it all away. So Wesakicak went hunting again even though he felt really tired. As he was walking, the lice started to talk to him. They said, "Wesakicak, you shouldn't have to go hunting again. You are tired. You should tell your wife not to give the meat away. You should keep it for yourself. You have to take care of yourself. Then the lice went back to sucking Wesakicak's blood and spitting poison into him. That was the reason Wesakicak was tired in the first place, because of the lice.

Well, anyway, Wesakicak got a Deer and brought it home. But this time he told his wife not to give the meat away. She looked at Wesakicak like there must be something wrong with him. When he ate and went to sleep she went out and gave away all the meat again. When Wesakicak woke up this time he was angry because she did not listen to him. She looked at Wesakicak again, like there must be something wrong with him. Then she saw the lice. 'Wesakicak, you have lice,' she said. 'Sit down here and I'll pick them off for you.' 'No,' said Wesakicak. 'They are my friends, they tell me things.' Well, Wesakicak listened to those lice and the things they told him while he was asleep. They told him that he should try to live like them. Just feed off other people. The lice did not have to go hunting. They did not have to feed the whole camp. They just ate and got fat and laid eggs and ate some more. Wesakicak should try to be like them, then he would not have to go out hunting when he was tired. So Wesakicak tried to get the other people in the camp to feed him and hunt for him. But the people just laughed. They thought Wesakicak was being silly. Of course a person has to look after themself and if they have extra they should share, but they can't lay around and expect others to look after them. Well, Wesakicak listened to those lice, to him they made sense. They sounded really smart and they certainly were fat and didn't have to work. The last I heard Wesakicak went to work for the World Trade Organization."

Harold's story might not have been the most traditional. But it had me chuckling long after I dropped him off and continued hunting. My scalp felt a little itchy though. The road wound down past the old community of Molanosa, the reconstructed Timber Bay with new houses and the ancient Evangelical Children's home, and the Reserve at the South end of Montreal Lake. Thunder was riding nice. The gas gauge had not moved since Wesley tapped it. I shook my thermos. It sounded with a promising swirl. There were still lots of Cheezies in the bag. So when I reached the pavement of highway #2, I turned South. It felt good to be on the road. I felt good. Thunder felt good. After the rattle and washboard of the old highway, the pavement felt good. I pulled the shifter down to third gear and Thunder hummed.

It had been years, but I remembered that there was good hunting down near Fort LaCorne. I think it was my buddy Dave Gaudry who told me, or maybe it was his brother, I can't remember. When the Metis first got back their hunting rights, I was hunting with Dave and his brother, we were trying to decide where to go. Someone suggested Fort LaCorne and Dave or his brother said, "There's more lights at night in Fort LaCorne than in Las Vegas." It wasn't long after that the province outlawed spotlights. Well, they outlawed spotlights for hunting. You can still buy a million candlepower light at Canadian Tire for fifteen bucks.

I had a new one behind the seat. My little brother, Robert, bought it for me; gave it to me wrapped in the white plastic bag from the store. "Here, Charlie, something for you." It wasn't Christmas or my birthday. Robert was just walking through the store, saw something, and because he had money in his pocket and didn't want to leave the store empty handed, he bought it. Robert likes to shop.

I stopped Thunder on the side of the road at the memory of that light back there. I brought it out, opened the cardboard box, removed the Styrofoam package and pulled out the big bulb with a pistol grip, and a lens as big as a small plate. I pulled the trigger and blinded myself. A million candles are bright. It hurt. I put the spotlight back. That was too painful to use on a Moose or Deer. As I was putting it back in the plastic bag I found the receipt. I was too blind to read it clearly, all I could make out was the price. Fifteen dollars. I fumbled in the bag again and found a handful of Canadian Tire money. I put the bills in my shirt pocket. I'd count it later when I could see.


WESAKICAK'S MOCCASINS BEAT A STEADY RHYTHM against the marble steps as he walked slowly down the stairs. He was looking for a place to finish the little nap he started and had cut short by Adonis' toe. This was a quiet place, a forgotten place. The only sound was the *wolp, wolp* of his moccasins. Well, going down was easier than going up. He would find some place at the bottom, a tree, maybe some shade, grass would be nice, lean back, close his eyes and dream.

"Behold, a barbarian." The purple-robed man sitting on the stairs put his doll aside. "Come barbarian, sit here a while and converse with me." He turned to the man sitting a few steps below. "This will be interesting." The lower man picked up his lap top computer and set it on his knees."

"Sit, sit, Barbarian. You and I will have a debate. No not there. Move down a couple of steps. A free man should not have to look up at a barbarian." Wesakicak complied by sliding his butt down the steps. "There, that's better. Now for the record, I am Socrates and the scribe there is Plato, and your name is . . . ?"

"Wesakicak"

"Wesakicak, What kind of name is that? Well no matter, we can expect barbarians to have strange names or else they would not be barbarians. Now, Barbarian," Socrates spread his hands. "I correct myself. Wesakicak. I should call you by your name for the sake of courtesy — for the sake of debate we will elevate you to the rank of a human. You have just come down from the towers of intrigue and petty gossip. Tell us, Wesakicak, what have you learned?"

Wesakicak leaned into the edge of the step behind him, leaned harder into it until it stretched out the ache in his muscles. Plato looked up from the screen in anticipation, his fingers on the keys. Socrates picked up his doll and set it on his lap.

"What kind of berries are those?" Wesakicak pointed his chin toward a bowl beside Socrates.

"These? These are olives. Would you like some?" He held the bowl out to Wesakicak. "Truly a barbarian, not to know the food of civilization," he remarked aside to Plato.

"These are like wild plums. They have a stone." Wesakicak tried one of the green ones. At first he wanted to spit, but that would not be polite. The fruit became more palatable as he nibbled the flesh from the pit. Not bad. He tried another.

"You see, Plato, the barbarian is always starving, never learned the art of cultivation and hence civilization. He follows the illusions and shadows of the forest and believes he understands the world. Tell me, Barbarian, what reason have you?"

Wesakicak spat a pit, fired the stone from between his teeth a good distance, wiggled his cheeks and fired another, and another, and another, and another, and finally spoke around the remaining stones in his mouth.

"My reason is to help Charlie," he gurgled.

"No, no, I did not mean your purpose, I meant your thoughts, your reason. You do reason, do you not?"

"My thoughts? You ask me my thoughts? My thoughts about what?"

"Now we are getting somewhere. Tell me your thoughts about the purpose of man. Why are we here? What is our greatest achievement?"

Wesakicak spat the few remaining stones, reached again for the bowl, but Socrates pulled it back. "Well, I guess the purpose of man is to live." Wesakicak snatched at the bowl, grabbed a handful, and sat back.

"To live. Very good, very good, perhaps we can converse, you and I. Now tell me, how shall we live?"

"We shall live," Wesakicak stalled, wriggled a few olive pits forward, spat, spat again, then continued. "We shall live like a family."

"Like a family? Do you mean we shall have a father figure in the lead, an eldest son, younger sons and then the rest following?"

"No, not like that. We should treat everyone as relatives with none above the other."

"None above the other. But how would you be organized? Who would be responsible?"

"Everyone should be responsible."

"Yes, yes, everyone responsible, granted, but who would make the decisions? Surely you would not allow women and the feeble minded to decide for themselves."

"Who would decide for them?"

"In a civilized state, only the intelligent, the worthy, the very best minds would make the important decisions. Women and the feeble minded must learn to obey."

Plato paused in his typing, struck a final key, waited while the compact printer buzzed a sheet of paper through, waited for the buzz to finish, pulled the sheet the rest of the way out, held it up and let it float away on the wind. He answered Wesakicak's quizzical look. "It is how we converse with the world."

Wesakicak tilted his head, still puzzled.

"The people read our words. They keep us alive here. For twenty centuries and more they have read our words. The word is the thing."

"So, if the people stop reading your words . . . "

"We fade into nothingness."

"You don't go up the steps to the top of the mountain?"

"Who would wish to? There is no intelligence up there, a clique of incestuous gossips, caught up in their own pettiness. You will find no insights on Mount Olympus." Plato readjusted the computer on his lap.

"You don't honour your forefathers?"

"They are not forefathers of ours." Socrates re-entered the conversation. "They only exist because the poets immortalized them. They have nothing to offer. In a perfect state there would be no need for the gods and especially not for the women among them."

"It appears to me, that you do not like women?" Wesakicak tried out formal speech. It did not fit his tongue, which at this time wriggled around olive flesh and pit. He spat. "What of your Mother? Your Grandmother?"

"Old women." Socrates bounced the doll on his knee. "They have a place in society. They are, after all, needed for procreation, but little more than that. They should be kept comfortable. But imagine if we allowed them into politics. Where would we be? It would lower the level of debate to the point where it would not be worth participating in any longer."

"You don't talk to your Mother?"

"Nor my father. It is the youth that we must communicate with. The youth with minds like clean slates upon which we inscribe ideas." Socrates patted the head of the doll. The doll smiled, turned adoring eyes up at the bearded face and buried his head in Socrates' shoulder. "You see, Wesakicak, if it were not for the youth, through these last long centuries, reading our words, we would not be here to debate with you. We would have faded into the dark of nothingness."

"What about your other place, that Hades place?"

"As my dear Plato here has said, we were saved from that forgotten place by our words. We are written here, Gutenberged here. We are always up to date. Hades has faded from memory, it barely exists now. We have exceeded that fate, surpassed it. We are forever."

"But surely," Wesakicak's tongue was getting into the rhythm of the conversation. "Your ideas must get old."

"Not at all. That is the beauty of it. So long as the conversation continues exclusively with the youth, our ideas will remain perpetually young. We are always modern."

"Don't you worry that you might lead them wrong."

"I deny that accusation." Socrates hugged the little boy. "I am not a corrupter of youth. I am their saviour. I have had enough of this foolish talk. Away with you now, Barbarian." Socrates clamped his mouth firmly shut. Plato closed the laptop. Wesakicak spread his hands questioning. "What did I say?"

Silence.

"Come now, we have just begun to visit." Wesakicak looked longingly at the bowl of olives.

The boy climbed down from Socrates' knee, gave Wesakicak a foul look, and walked away. Socrates followed, head high. Plato tucked the laptop under one arm and the bowl of olives under the other, shook his head at Wesakicak, as if to say "you are a pitiful person" and followed Socrates and the boy. They all walked stiffly with straight backs like people who have been insulted and want to show that they still have dignity.

Wesakicak sat a while on the marble steps and thought to himself, "Oh well, those funny little fruit didn't taste that good." And went to see if maybe Charlie Muskrat was a Christian.

I WAS STILL HUNTING WHEN I made the turn from the old gravel road onto the highway heading South, thinking maybe a Moose or even an Elk might come out of the National Park and cross this bit of pavement that ran down close to the Park's eastern border. There was a chance of meat this way. Suddenly, someone ran out of the trees and stuck out his thumb. There sure were lots of hitchhikers for a cold March morning. I skidded Thunder to a stop.

"Winston Zack on my way to P.A. Glad for the ride."

"I'm Charlie Muskrat from up near Lac La Ronge."

"So, Charlie, are you a Christian?" Winston asked without even catching his breath

"I never thought much about it." I tried to be vague. I didn't want to insult Winston. Christians could be touchy when they weren't being pushy. Some Christians were pretty cool, those who didn't preach and walked in a good way, all smiles and glad times.

"Listen to this." Winston dug around in his parka and pulled out a black album of CDs. He thumbed through the box set and slid a CD in the dash player. Thunder must have came with a CD player because I never put one in, and honestly, I didn't remember seeing it before. That's no surprise.

*Johnny Cash, Unearthed — Volume Four, My Mother's Hymn Book*, and it sounded good. It sounded real good. "Where We'll Never Grow Old", "I Shall Not Be Moved". I eased back into the seat and drove old Thunder left handed, a cup of coffee in my right and listened. "Do Lord, oh do Lord, do remember me, way beyond the Blue." My foot began to tap and Thunder rocked down the line, picked up speed with Johnny's picking. The needle bounced between a hundred ten and a hundred twenty.

I looked over and smiled at Winston, he was watching me intently. I nodded, he nodded back. Johnny can sure sing. "I'll fly away oh glory, I'll fly away, when I die hallelujah by and by, I'll fly away." Thunder hummed along. Winston smiled, I smiled, I nodded, Winston nodded. "To Canaan's land. I'm on my way, where the soul of man never dies. My darkest night will turn to day, where the soul of man never dies . . . where all is peace and joy and love . . . where the soul of man never dies." You have to admit Johnny can bring those old songs to life even though it sounds like he was wishing for his own end.

Thunder slowed when Johnny slowed, surged with new energy when Johnny sang "In the sweet by and by we shall meet on that beautiful shore." We barely made eighty when Johnny sang "Come home, Come home, ye who are weary come home." When the CD ended we sat quiet with the last words still echoing in the cab of the truck. "I come, just as I am, I come."

"So what do you think of that?" Winston asked.

"Pretty damn good."

"But did it speak to your heart?"

"I have to admit, I don't much listen to hymns but, when Johnny sings, I think everyone listens."

"Well how about this?" and Winston replaced the CD with *Volume Five*. "Delia's gone one more round Delia's gone. She was low down and trifling . . . First time I shot her I shot her in the side, hard to watch her suffer, but with the second shot she died." I nodded, Winston nodded, we rode old Thunder down the asphalt "like a bird on a wire". "Bad luck wind been blowing on my back." Thunder got into it again. "Got the number thirteen tattooed on my neck." We really rocked down the line when Johnny sang "Gonna break my rusty cage and run." "I'm burn'n diesel, I'm burn'n dinosaur bones." The needle bounced with my tapping foot. We roared through Northside without notice. I felt Winston watch me. I smiled and nodded.

"There's a man going round taking names." Made the hairs on my arms stand up, a shiver through my spine. Thunder rocked. Winston nodded, I nodded. "and the whirlwind is in the thorn trees." I felt a lump rise in my throat and I turned away from Winston just in case a tear snuck out. "when the man comes around."

The CD ended as we crossed the North Saskatchewan River and entered Prince Albert.

"Which do you like better?" Winston asked.

"Which what?" I asked still a little choked.

"The first one or the last one."

"Well, everyone knows that Johnny can sing gospel, but man when he sings songs like 'I hurt myself today to see if I still feel, I focused on the pain the only thing that's real.' Like in that last song, you have to admit that he is much more than a gospel singer. The man has something to say to everyone."

"Let me out here." Winston ejected his CD and put it back in the black album. "You know Charlie, if you were a Christian things would be a lot simpler." And then he was gone.

And there I was in Prince Albert with a 30/30 Winchester under the seat, half a tank of gas, half a thermos of coffee and lots of Cheezies. I have to admit it has been a long time since I went South as far as Prince Albert. It's not that I dislike cities. I just like to be home with Wendy. There is something about home, even when it is just the two of us, something that draws me back that makes me laugh and act goofy. I keep Beverly laughing. Or

I try to keep her laughing. Mostly she just smiles, that smile that says "Charlie, you're a nut." I wanted to turn around and go home right then and there but I saw a MacDonald's sign.

Now the thing about Beatrice is that she does not let me eat greasy food. I like everything fried in lard. Everything. One time when she was out picking berries and I was home alone and apt to get into her kitchen even though I don't know where anything is, I found some bologna and a pound of shortening. Heaven in a sandwich. She was not home five minutes and she knew what I had done. My neck hurt from walking around with my head down. It was days and days of, "Charlie, I just want you to live a long, long time, and you know there is heart disease in your family, and you know, and you know, and you know, and I love you, Charlie, and I want to live with you when we are old. You promised me, Charlie, that we would grow old together, don't you remember?"

"Uh huh"

"Tell me again what you said that afternoon."

"Don't you remember?"

"I remember, I just want to hear it again."

Laughs, hugs, kisses, and smiles.

Well, she would not find out about the Quarter Pounder.

MacDonald's is not like the last time I was there. The lineups are shorter to start with. All of a sudden I was in front of a very young woman behind a till. The menu behind her was a lot larger than I remembered: salads and breakfast, and Big Macs, and Filet-O-Fish, and chicken, and wraps, and veggie wraps, and, oh yeah, they still make a Quarter Pounder.

"With cheese?" the very young woman asked.

"And lard?"

She looked at me.

"Yes, with cheese, please."

"Would you like that super sized?"

"Oh yeah."

Oh yeah, and fries, lots of fries, and the clown smiled, and I smiled, and the seats are not hard plastic anymore. A quarter pound of pure beef, no muscle or gristle, and tastes like it was fried in pure lard. The bun, now there is an invention that our cousins the Caucasians can be proud of. They crisp-fry it so that it soaks up all the grease and we all know that the grease is what makes it all work. Their next greatest invention is the deep fryer. In that bubbling cauldron of magic everything can be made to taste like a MacDonald's french-fry. Elizabeth says they live in a french-fry society. You can explain everything about them through the french-fry. Don't like the taste of fish? Dip it in batter, and boil it in grease. She says that's why Pickerel are so expensive, and Whitefish prices keep going down. Pickerel are naturally dry and tasteless, they go good in grease. She says if we ever wanted to be rich, all we had to do was figure out how to deep fry money. I pushed thoughts of my beautiful wife aside and enjoyed my decadence with cheese.

I took the road South from Prince Albert, the idea of hunting at Fort La Corne was behind me. St. Louis on the South Saskatchewan River waits on the far side of a narrow iron bridge. River Road runs South and West from St. Louis, past Batoche and Almighty Voice bluff. History Road would be a better name. This is the territory where the invaders attacked the Metis, where the Mounties dragged a cannon out of Prince Albert, set it up on a hill and used it on Almighty Voice and a couple of his friends. Almighty Voice's crime was that he killed one of his cows without the permission of the Indian Agent.

Thunder rolled gently through the flowing hills. It was as though he was hunting as he moved gracefully through the corners. The rifle rested on the seat beside me. It had been years since I travelled this road. Memories tried to find their way into my mind and I caught glimpses of them but they were mostly shadow, swirls in the bottom of a wine bottle.

My stomach was doing strange things. It groaned and moaned and turned. I poured coffee into it to ease the twist. That didn't help. I drove a while in agony and waited for the action to slow. As Thunder crested a rise, three white-tail Deer lifted their heads. Thunder slowed to a stop without skidding on the gravel. A well-trained hunting truck. I quietly opened the door, and slid out ahead of my rifle. The Deer stood down a slope in an open field. A buck stood broadside, an easy shot, a gift. He stood there, an offering, his flesh to feed my sister-in-law. Not as much meat as a Moose, but more than enough to fill several plates and pots of stew.

I am very happy that I never pulled the trigger. A 30/30 rifle has a good kick to it. As it was, I barely made it into the trees with a handful of paper towel snatched from under the seat before my stomach let loose.

The need to stop and run into the trees occasionally followed me all that day. I could not go home. Esther would know that I had indulged in grease and I still needed to bring home meat.

My stomach churned as I rode Thunder down River Road. At Gabriel's Crossing I stopped to see if Maria was home. She wasn't, but there was a fresh roll of toilet paper in her outhouse that I borrowed. Maria would understand. She grew up on wild meat. Knew the hazards of hunting.

As I turned onto highway 11, I was surprised to see another hitchhiker. It was like I was back in 1967, there were so many thumbs on the road. Mind you, back in '67, it was usually my thumb wind burned on the highway.

"Name's Whelan. Thanks for the lift."

"Where you headed, Whelan?" I purposely used his name so that it would stay in my memory longer.

"Today, I'm going to Saskatoon."

I didn't ask where he was going tomorrow. I played Whelan the Johnny Cash CDs that Winston left in the truck and we rode together in reverent silence as the "singer of songs" serenaded us. I caught Whelan looking at me. I looked back, he nodded, I nodded, my stomach churned and rolled over. Something about the way Whelan looked at me reminded me of Winston and Wesley.

"You need to eat." Whelan suggested.

"Naw, I don't think food will help. I'll just have to wait this out."

"Soup," Whelan stated. "Soup will fix that. I know a place in Saskatoon where they serve the best soup."

I left Thunder at the Queen Elizabeth power station at Whelan's persistence and we caught a ride into the city with a power plant worker just coming off shift. Whelan's persistence was a simple "Trust me." I had nothing better at mind. I wasn't going to be hunting for a while.

"Soup." Whelan pointed to the Friendship Inn as we walked together down 20th Street. The Friendship Inn was around when I was in my wander years. Thirty years ago, most of the clients were hippies. The beards and bell-bottoms and braids left years ago. Today the Friendship Inn serves Indians. The neighbourhood changed like an ecological transformation. One species moved out and another moved in, attracted by the niche of accessible habitat. Parasite slumlords feed off whichever people are drawn to their territory. Today the hippies who once resisted, form the core of the establishment. They are the teachers and social workers. The psuedo-hippies who just went along to smoke dope are still smoking dope.

The soup was good, plenty of meat, and large chunks of vegetables. The bread was bakery leftover, old and dry. I ate like everyone else, quietly. It doesn't matter how long a person accepts domination and dependence, when the food is a gift, people take it with humility. Most people simply ate quietly and left.

A few people sat around to visit. Whelan was a very accomplished visitor. He made visiting into an art form. I sat back with a coffee and appreciated my travelling companion's skill as he told stories, teased, drew a story out of a near elder, gently teased a woman into blushing and played with a bold child who climbed onto his lap.

The people all eventually left and I followed Whelan into the social worker's office. He seemed to want to prolong his visit. At first I felt sorry for the busy worker. Whelan seemed to me to be an interruption. To Sherry, Whelan was a client and clients were her business. I watched Whelan visit and I have to admit that he is one of the best. In the North the visit has definite form, though it is never formal. Whelan made the visit more than form. He added substance to it.

Sherry was drawn into Whelan's visit and soon began to give us information. There are things that happen in the core of the big prairie town that never make it into the news. Saskatoon and Saskatchewan hide their eyes, the CBC is deaf and blind and dumb. Commissions and enquiries meet in downtown hotels and drink Starbucks coffee. There is one person in Saskatoon who knows what's going on and she is nearly burned out from trying to maintain hope.

I felt a deep sadness as we left the Friendship Inn. "I didn't know," I stated flatly to Whelan.

"Now you do."

"What do you mean?"

"You did not know, now you do."

"I guess so. But what do I do about it?"

"That's up to you. Cry about it. Scream about it, forget it, but now you cannot say that you did not know."

We walked in silence on the ice-crusted sidewalk. The free needles that various agencies gave out to prevent AIDS were beginning to show where the snow and ice melted. By spring they would all be visible and available for children to play with. Another fix that turned into a fuck up. I wondered whether I could do better. If any of my ideas might result in change that did not turn into another problem.

"How do we get back to the truck?" I asked Whelan.

"That's easy." Whelan stepped ahead of me and began staggering down the street. He bounced off a sign and fell into a store entrance, picked himself up and stumbled on down the street. I followed and chuckled at Whelan's clown. It was a good clown. He played the drunk Indian perfectly.

Then I was in the back of a police car, face down, with my hands cuffed behind me. There was a lump behind my ear that throbbed and fought for my attention. I didn't want to pay attention to it. I wanted to see where I was going and eventually wriggled myself into a sitting position. The two police officers on the other side of the plexiglass partition were silent, stoic. Whelan was nowhere in sight.

The police car came to a stop. The officer who had been driving opened the back door, grabbed me by the collar and pulled me out of the car. He took back his handcuffs and drove away. I looked around, pulled myself together and walked fifty feet to Thunder. Now how did those police officers know that I had left my truck out by the power station?

I felt under my shirt. The little leather bag full of white pebbles was still there. The gas gauge still showed half a tank, the thermos still sounded a swirl, and the Cheezies bag was still half full. I pulled the rifle out from behind the seat of the truck and drove toward the rising full moon. I imagined a Moose silhouetted against the bright silver circle, an easy shot in the night against the white of spring snow. I remember when the Saskatchewan government outlawed night hunting. Nothing changed much for me or the people that I know in the North. We continue to hunt at night, especially when the moon is full. In early winter when there are only a few hours of daylight, governmental regulation just doesn't matter. I worried for a moment about whether they might take night hunting more serious down here on the prairie. Then I let the thought dissipate into the darkness. It was just too much effort.

I drove a long while without seeing anything edible. Slowly the night drew my strength. I began to feel drowsy. Thunder is not the most comfortable truck to sleep in. An old sleeping bag behind the seat, one of those just-in-case things, just in case the truck breaks down, just in case the heater quits, just in case Lori wants to sleep on the way home late at night, or just in case I need something to wrap around groceries to keep the lettuce from freezing. I wrapped it around me, my parka for a pillow, and I slept like a baby until daylight showed over the dash.

WESAKICAK WATCHED THE MIST SWIRL IN front and around his moccasins. He was nowhere. Nowhere is a good place to be when you are trying to think. There are no distractions. Wesakicak looked up from his feet at the nothing that surrounded him. He turned full circle. Still nothing. Nothing in front or behind. No distractions, but no inspiration either. What to do about Charlie? Wesakicak had no ideas. He walked onward not going anywhere. He waved at the mist in front of his eyes, tried to clear his vision, tried to see.

"I need inspiration," he said to the nothing.

Nothing answered with a song.

Wesakicak stopped, not that he was going anywhere anyway, and listened.

The song was sweet and gentle and pulled Wesakicak toward the right. The mist thinned slightly as he walked through the nothing toward the song. The women sat in a circle of the nothing and created music that pushed against the nothing. The music eased the mist aside and left the women in a clearing. Wesakicak wondered if they had food.

"Only for the soul," one woman answered.

"What do you feed a spirit?" Wesakicak asked.

"Art."

"And where does art come from?" Wesakicak wondered whether it might be a particular cut, like Moose ribs or Beaver tail.

"Art comes from us. We create it and share it with the mortals."

"And who are you?" Wesakicak really wanted to know who they were related to.

"We are the Muses of legend."

Wesakicak did not know where legend was. Maybe it was close to Molanosa. "Do you know Charlie Muskrat?" he asked.

"Is he an artist?"

"He could be, I guess."

"Does he sing, or paint, or write, or tell stories, or sculpt?"

"No, he is a hunter, a good hunter."

The Muses put their heads together and whispered. They whispered a long time and Wesakicak started to get hungry thinking about if Charlie got the Moose he was after.

"We agree that hunting might be an art. Usually art is shared . . ."

"Charlie shares the meat ..." Wesakicak interrupted. He normally would not interrupt anyone who was talking. But he had discovered in his "debates" on Mount Olympus that interruptions could be used strategically.

"He has to share the art, not the product. If Charlie Muskrat wants our help, then he must first seek our help, then ask our help, then give something important in exchange for our help. We will make Charlie the greatest hunter in all time if Charlie cuts off his ears."

"But how will he hear a Moose walking in soft snow if he has no ears?"

"Then he can cut off his nose."

"But how will he smell an Elk in rut?"

"Then he can cut off his penis."

Wesakicak walked away. Next time he saw Charlie Muskrat he would warn him about the Muses. Their help was way too expensive.


"LILITH." I RECOGNIZED HER RIGHT OFF. "Why are you coming to me? I'm married." She sat above me, straddled me, her bare breasts large and smooth and upturned. She shook her head so that her long brown hair swirled around her shoulders. The Church calls Lilith a demon, comes to steal the seed of men. Joyce warned me about her, said she only comes to single men or men away from their wives. She said Lilith was Adam's first wife, before Eve.

"You are not married, Charlie." Lilith leaned closer. I could smell her breath, fresh saliva, natural, normal. "You cannot even remember her name."

"Just because I have a poor memory doesn't mean I can't be married."

"You have a good memory, Charlie. You remember my name. You remember every time we have been together."

That was true. Lilith dreams do not fade in the morning. Lilith rides a man's mind during the day as she rode his body during the night.

"I remember you, Lilith. I have good memories of you. I remember every visit. I used to think you came from Mother Earth because we always met someplace clean and green, like that time in the trees and I listened to the sound of a river flowing over stones. But I am married now and you should leave me alone."

"You are not married, Charlie, not in a church or with a pipe. You never promised *Kakiki Mina Kakiki* to anyone."

I felt her hand search between us, felt her take my hardness in her fist. I wondered whether it was really an act of unfaithfulness to be with another woman in a dream. I remembered my home, log walls, stairs made from logs, a loft, and a bed, Jenny sleeping alone.

Lilith let go, stood, and began to dress. "You are married, Charlie. Never forget that, and never forget me. Take care of your manliness." She reached down, took me in her fist again and pecked a kiss upon the tip. "Never trade this for anything, dear Charlie, it is half the balance of all things living."

When I awoke Thunder was cold. I wasn't, but I soon would be if Thunder didn't start. "Please, Buddy, please start." I tromped the gas pedal twice. Thunder whined a long whine, coughed, whined again, caught and hummed. "Thanks, Buddy." There was light in the East. When Thunder warmed up, we headed that way just to see what was there. You can sometimes surprise a Moose at daybreak.

It is hard to imagine anything alive on the Saskatchewan prairie on a cold stark March morning. Westwind followed Thunder and me as we sailed along the highway. Snow swirled under and around our tires. A semi-trailer truck raised a cloud of billowing white as we met. I really didn't want to shoot a Moose this morning, even if I could drive Thunder close. The skinning and cutting process would be an endurance test in that wind.

"It's damn cold out there, Buddy." I began a conversation with Thunder. "Even if I could keep my hands warm from the Moose's body heat, it wouldn't be fun." Thunder is easy to talk to. He never interrupts. A good listener. The problem is he never answers. So I continued the conversation with myself.

"Thelma wants Moose meat."

"Maybe *she* should be out here hunting."

"Do you really want her along?"

"Probably not, too hard on Thunder's springs."

I chuckled at my little joke and patted the top of the steering wheel.

"Wouldn't need Thunder. Put an ox harness on her and she could drag a Moose back home."

The image wasn't funny and I let it fade. The prairie lay open around us and Thunder rolled down a blacktop stripe that split the flowing, drifting whiteness into North-South sections.

"Thelma intimidates you, doesn't she?" I was surprised by my question.

"What makes you say that?"

"It's just that you always put her down."

"I don't *always* put her down."

"Maybe not always, but often enough. When was the last time you said something nice about her?"

"I say lots of nice things about her."

"Like what?"

"Like, well, um, like she doesn't need a husband, she's man enough for two."

"That wasn't funny."

"Sure it was."

"No it wasn't."

"Who you arguing with?"

"You."

"But who are you?"

"You."

"This is stupid. I'm not talking to you anymore."

"Then *who* are you talking to?"

"Nobody."

"Thelma *does* intimidate you. Doesn't she?"

"Get off it, will ya. Thelma is a big, big woman. I feel sorry for her."

"Why?"

"Why? Why do you have to ask? Think about it."

"You haven't."

"Haven't what?"

"Thought about it."

"Who the hell is arguing with me?"

"You are."

"This is stupid."

"You said that already."

"And it's still stupid."

"You're the one who's arguing."

WESAKICAK TURNED BACK TO THE MUSES. Maybe there was something here. Maybe not. He had nothing better to do and besides they had nice legs. Those short white skirts showed a lot of flesh. Wesakicak respected women. His mother was a woman, so were his sisters, all of them. It was just that when that much attractive leg was exposed to his sight Wesakicak had trouble putting his man thoughts aside.

"Do you know Charlie's story?" Wesakicak asked. He forced himself to look into her eyes and not down to where the short skirt ended and flesh began.

"It hasn't been told yet."

"Who is going to tell it?"

"Charlie is."

"What about Harold Johnson?"

"Charlie will tell Harold."

"When?"

"As it happens."

"Do you know the ending?"

"How could I know the ending until the ending happens?" She was indignant. "We know who you are, Wesakicak. There are many many stories about you."

"Who told you."

"You did."

"I'm not a storyteller."

"You told your story as you lived it, Wesakicak. You are a fiction."

"Are you a fiction?"

"No, we are real, Wesakicak. Only mythical people are fiction."

"If I am a fiction because I lived for a long, long time, why are you not fictions too?"

She shook her head in disbelief. "We are real, Wesakicak. Look at us, touch us. Can't you see that we are real?"

"Why am I a fiction then? You can see me, you can touch me."

"You are a fiction, Wesakicak, because you are made up. People make up stories about you. Like the time you tricked the animals. That never happened. Those are just stories people use to explain how things came to be and you are blamed for it."

"But I did trick the animals. Lots of times."

"Come on, Wesakicak, we are the Muses. You can't fool us. You are a fiction and we are real."

Wesakicak sat down in the mist cross-legged and rubbed his sore feet. If he was a fiction why did his feet hurt? He thought for a long time and eavesdropped on the Muses' conversation. They seemed to be arguing about who was the greatest painter of all time? Who was the greatest poet? Wesakicak listened for a while then fell asleep. It all seemed to go nowhere.


It began to rain as I approached Winnipeg. Freezing rain that glazed Highway 1 and shimmered the pavement. March weather can be anything, and usually is something. I let Thunder find his own speed and he slowed as we approached the perimeter highway. The light changed from yellow to red and I gently pressed the brake. Thunder did not slow and I pressed a little harder. Thunder slid slightly to the left and I eased up on the pedal. Damn ice.

Suddenly he was in front of me with his broom, sweeping frantically. People on the sidewalk were yelling "SWEEP, SWEEP." I pressed hard on the brake pedal and Thunder turned a complete 360 degrees and came to a stop exactly on the thick, white stop line that showed clearly through the transparent ice. I breathed again.

The sweeper in his colourful wool sweater and tam slid on one foot, pushing with the other across the intersection and began to sweep frantically in front of a Peterbuilt pulling a reefer trailer. The huge truck slowly rotated in a big jack-knifed loop. As it slid completely through the intersection, I caught a glimpse of the driver and his expression could only mean one thing. "Oh, shit."

The crowd on the sidewalk cheered as the Peterbuilt completed a full rotation, its wheels locked and sliding. The sweeper held his broom over his head with both hands in a "hurrah" for himself. Someone on the sidewalk poured himself a glass of whiskey from a bottle in a brown paper bag. Street curling. A new dimension to an old game, an extreme sport. I wondered whether it would catch on as the light turned green and Thunder eased through the intersection.

Rebecca walked to the bus stop, sat on the cold metal bench in the glass shelter, out of the wind, with her book. She had plenty of time this morning having left her apartment early. It was not that she was eager to get to university, but rather that she was embarrassed out of her home. Her Mother came to visit. That was a good thing. Rebecca liked the memories of home that her mother brought to the city. She also liked it that her mother cooked for her. Smoked fish soup for supper last night. Rebecca could still taste the delicate smoky flavour that permeated the soup, and memories of the North flooded back.

This morning Rebecca's mother wanted to make bannock and asked Rebecca if she had baking powder. Rebecca proudly brought out a huge can. One of those bargains she found at one of those bulk food stores that only exist on the outskirts of cities where normally an Indian from the inner city cannot afford the transportation to shop at. Her mother beamed her pride at her daughter. Such a huge can. Her daughter kept tradition here in the city.

Then her mother asked for flour and Rebecca was forced to bring out the two-pound bag from the convenience store down the street. Beside the can of baking powder, the bag of flour seemed ridiculously small. Her mother never said anything. There was no need. The disappointment clearly showed. Rebecca then made the excuse that she had to go to class to get away from the embarrassment.

She found her place in the book she was reading, the one the weird boy in her class had given her, trying to impress her. Flipping pages with her mitts on proved difficult. She read about a man with a poor memory in an old truck he named Thunder, out on an adventure. She was intrigued by the diamonds he wore in a leather bag tied around his neck.

Traffic moved slowly in front of her, a parade of humanity encased in steel and glass — cars, vans, SUVs. She looked down the street for her bus and there he was looking at her, an Indian in an old truck. Charlie Muskrat? The thought jumped into her mind. She looked down at the book in her hand, then back up. Sure, why not? That could be Charlie Muskrat. She waved, gave the man a big smile as he drove slowly past, followed traffic, slid, stopped, spun tires, moved, braked, slid down the street.

I turned Thunder left on Broadway and we drove gently through the University area following the route of the Trans-Canada eastward. After listening to the only news about Winnipeg that made it onto CBC, I expected to see gangs of Indians, red bandanas and guns. Maybe it was too early in the morning.

A young woman in a bus shelter smiled and waved at me. I smiled and waved back, wondered if I knew her. Was I supposed to remember her name? Not likely. My little leather bag tied around my neck felt heavy in that moment, like it was reminding me it was there.

I turned Thunder South as we left Winnipeg and headed for North Dakota. I wasn't really going anywhere. I just let Thunder wander and he headed South. Why not? South can be a good direction in the winter.

The uniformed man at the border was not impressed by an Indian with braids and no money. "Do you have a gun?" he asked me.

"Well, not a hand gun." I didn't want to tell anyone I was road hunting.

"You need a hand gun to enter the US." He hoisted up his belt with both hands, but his belly pushed it back down. Or maybe the weight of the 44-magnum, long barrel, Clint Eastwood Dirty Harry special on his hip pulled the belt back down. "How are you going to defend freedom, son, unless you have a hand gun?" I looked closer at the border guard. No, he wasn't my dad. I remained silent.

"Do you have a bible?"

"I'm sorry, no. But I have Johnny Cash's mother's hymn book on CD." I added quickly, hopefully.

"Not good enough, son." I looked again to see if this man was my father. He still wasn't. "If you do not have a passport, you need a hand gun and a bible to enter the home of the free and the land of the brave. Sorry, son, you will have to turn back."

Thunder U-turned in a single lane and sped back North. He seemed afraid. We eased down around Dryden and stopped for a break. Or a brake stopped us. One of Thunder's brake shoes picked up a stone or something, I figured, because it really squeaked when I pressed the pedal. I don't like to see Thunder hurting so I pulled into a dealership to talk about maybe fixing whatever might be wrong. I had a few dollars in my pocket, but not nearly the amount demanded by the dealership. And they would not release Thunder until I paid them the hundred and twenty bucks they demanded for pulling off a rear wheel and brake drum to check for a stone.

I walked through the dismal town, with its pulp mill effluent so thick it moistened the air. I stopped in a restaurant for a coffee and sandwich and pondered my plight. What the hell was I going to do? I didn't have the money. I had no way of getting the money. I was stuck on the Trans-Canada and they knew it. The coffee and sandwich cost me thirteen dollars and I wondered what happened to the price of bread and butter. Maybe they paid the coffee-bean pickers a fair wage. Somehow I doubted it, and walked out into the dread of a smoky, overcast sky.

Thunder waited for me at the curb. Someone at the dealership must have forgot to hobble him. We rode away together laughing. Well I was laughing and Thunder seemed to be having the time of his life, until he passed that police car. Good thing in Canada you don't have to pay speeding tickets immediately or Thunder and I would still be in Ontario. After that we slowed down a bit, and headed for my buddy's namesake. Thunder Bay.

I like this part of Canada. They put up big signs for hunters that show the best places to hunt. Big signs with pictures of Moose on them. I didn't see any real Moose after our obligatory stop in Thunder Bay. I think even Thunder was bored there, and we drove on eastward.

I missed the turn-off to Toronto at Sudbury. I was changing CDs. I was really beginning to enjoy Johnny Cash. Anyway, we arrived in Ottawa the evening of March 31st. It was like nothing I'd ever seen before. Or maybe it was. San Diego when the sailors get paid is kind of like Ottawa on the 31st of March. But, instead of drunken sailors, I met weaving politicians and bureaucrats with arm loads of money, looking for friends.

"Charlie, are you my friend?"

"Sure."

"Here, take this money and help your people with it."

She stuffed my pocket with twenties.

"Thank you."

"No, thank the department of Indian Affairs. We have a surplus."

All evening, in every bar that I entered, politicians and bureaucrats gave me money because I looked Indian. Their reason was always the same, a surplus. Who was I to argue? The drinks were all free and the food was the best I had in a long time. Better than dry Cheezies. We ate filet mignon, and drank the best wine and later we drank 12-year-old scotch, and people kept giving me money.

I met this guy named Steve or Stephan or Steward or something, who assured me that Canada was in great shape, asked me if I was his friend and when I assured him I was, he gave me a whole bag full of money — new quarters minted that day with a picture of a real old lady on one side. It was an incredible night, drinking and partying and eating only the best food, and money everywhere. At midnight everyone went home, so I found Thunder again and my sleeping bag and went to sleep. The big bag of quarters did not make a good pillow, so I put it behind the seat.

The next morning I saw Steve, that was his name right? I wasn't sure. He was heading toward the hill. He still had bags full of money. I waved and crossed the street to say hello to the party animal. But he acted like he didn't know me.

"Sure Stephan, it's me, Charlie Muskrat. Remember last night in the pub? I'm your friend remember?"

Steve or Stephan or Stewart or whoever he was must have had a real hangover. He didn't remember me. He hugged his bags of money and scurried on to the hill. Confused, I followed along. I tried again. "Remember the surplus?"

"Young man, today is the first of April, the beginning of a new fiscal year. There is no surplus today." Stephan walked away stiffly, tightly holding onto his bags of money.

It felt good to be called a young man. I stood on the sidewalk in front of the Parliament Buildings and looked around. Everywhere, bureaucrats scurried with bags full of money, looking furtively over their shoulders to see if anyone was following them.

"Must be April Fool's day," I thought as I headed back toward where I had left Thunder. On the way I met nine old men and women wearing black robes. They played on the street in front of a stone building, the one with the wide steps and the heavy wooden doors. Two played hopscotch, one skipped while two others twirled the rope for her, three played marbles, knuckling glass shooters across the tiny lawn. The last black robe sat by herself with a deck of cards spread out on the step. I watched for a moment, kept my mouth shut deliberately, remembered Tracy's words. "If I ever get lost, I'll just sit down and play solitaire. Sure as anything, you or someone else will come along and tell me where the next card goes."

This black robe didn't need any help. She cheated. But who am I to say, maybe she played by her own rules.

"Psst, wanna see a trick?"

I turned around, another black robe held both his hands out toward me, fists clenched.

"Sure." What else could I say?

"Examine this." He opened a fist, palm up, showed me a tiny Indian.

"Yeah."

"Now examine this." He opened his other hand: a little scarlet RCMP officer, hat and everything looked up at me, saluted.

"Yeah."

"Indian cannot pursue a legal action against the officer because of the uniform."

"Uh huh"

"Now, if you will observe." He closed both hands. Opened them again. The little Indian was still there in one hand. The RCMP officer stood naked in the other. I turned my eyes away to spare him his shame.

"Now the Indian can initiate an action against the officer."

"Good trick."

"It is not over yet." The black robe closed his fists again. Opened them again. The Indian was still there, looking confused. The Mountie now wore a suit of plain clothes. Three lawyers stood with him, brief cases and everything.

"I don't get it."

"Indian may now file a statement of claim against the RCMP if he has a sufficient amount of money. Now, that's a trick."

I still didn't get it, but I smiled and nodded, remembered to be polite.

"Did you like that?"

"Not bad."

"It is not a classic. Do you remember the one we played on you in 1894?"

"No, can't say I was around back then."

"I was, honest, I was there. Fantastic. We snatched the earth right out from under your feet, the classic tablecloth trick expanded to a whole country. Now, that was magic. Certainly our best of all time, you should have seen it."

"Must've been something."

"Oh, it was. It was," the black robe who cheated at solitaire assured me. "That trick we called St. Catherine's Milling and the Queen." She nodded her head slowly, nostalgically. "Classic, pure classic. We do not get a chance for many of those these days. But you must see some of the stuff we do with the Charter. Did he show you the one about bringing an action against the police?"

"Yeah, I just saw that."

"That one is good, but it is not a classic."

"Hey, it's good to meet you guys, but I gotta go." I tried to get away.

"May we give you a hug? It is a rare opportunity to hug an Indian."

"I guess."

Her robes smelled musty as she wrapped her arms around me. The other eight took turns shaking my hand and hugging me. When they were done, my watch and my wallet were gone. The earth beneath my feet no longer felt real, like I might just sink away.

"What happened?" I asked.

"Nothing. Crown's honour," the chief black robe assured.

"Crown's honour?"

"Crown's honour," the other eight echoed.

"Come on, Charlie." I felt someone tug at my arm. It was Wesley Jack, dressed like one of those homeless people you see all over the place in these cities.

"Hey guys, gotta go." I waved at the black robes.

"Good bye, Charlie. Good bye, Charlie." They waved back as Wesley pulled me along.

"Hey Wesley, how come you're dressed like that?" I asked once he stopped urgently pulling at my arm.

"Invisibility."

"Really?"

"Yeah, dress like this and nobody can see you. They walk right past, can't even look at you. Powerful medicine."

"But I can see you."

"They couldn't."

"The black robes?"

"Yeah, them. Now Charlie, this is important. Stay away from them. Those are the Supreme Wizards. They got medicine. Dangerous medicine." Wesley shook his head, sadness showed on his face. "I seen what they done."

"You mean that 1894 trick. That Saint, what's her name and the Queen thing."

"Charlie." Wesley took me by both shoulders, stared into my face, serious. "They have power over all of the Earth. Wizards can make something out of nothing and nothing out of something."

"Okay, Wesley. I promise I won't go around them no more."

"I'm serious. Here's your watch and wallet." Wesley held them out to me.

"How'd you do that?"

"I'm a wizard too."


It looked like a church, ancient stone architecture, carefully swept drive, spires, and cold. The sun glinted off the green copper roofs. I was sure it was a church or a monastery. Anyway, it was Sunday and Thunder had stopped out front. He'd pulled off the big busy highway, turned into Kingston, and parked here. I sat behind the wheel and stared at the stone wall: maybe it was Disneyland. Naw, it had to be a church. I smoked a cigarette and wondered why Thunder would bring me here. I cracked the window a full inch and a half to let the smoke out. The wind from across Lake Ontario carried the smell of water. Spring would not be far. That was it! Thunder must have brought me here because it was Easter. An Easter Mass might be nice. For sure the food would be good. I can sing Christian. I can really sing Christian when there is food at the end.

I walked up to the gate. The guard said it wasn't a church, or a monastery, or Disneyland. He said it was a penitentiary — Collins Bay Penitentiary. Then he strip-searched me. That wasn't too bad, a little cold out there in the wind, but not nearly as bad as the cavity search. I wondered if this wasn't the last residential school maybe. I walked back to Thunder shaking my head. "What you bring me here for?" He didn't answer. I sat there a while totally bewildered, lit another cigarette, poured another a cup of coffee. I couldn't figure this out. Why a jail? What was he trying to tell me? I looked around. There was a big tree out the passenger window, an Oak, or an Elm maybe. I'd heard of them. I wasn't sure. We don't have those kind of trees in northern Saskatchewan, just Pine and Birch, Poplar and Spruce. Willow, but that's not a tree.

A man came out through the gate, and across the lane. He walked up to Thunder and I rolled down the window. When I saw the little white rectangle at his throat, I butted the cigarette. When I turned back to the window his hands rested on the rim. The old face above the black collar looked sad, even behind the smile.

"I understand you are looking for a church, my son."

"Uh huh, I guess."

"I am Father Theodore. I am the Chaplain here. Tell me, my son, why do you seek the Church?" The voice was as sad as the face, tired, though he tried to be enthusiastic.

"I'm not sure, my truck kinda brought me here."

"The Lord brought you here."

"He did?"

"He did."

I looked away from the Chaplain and around the cab. Who really brought me here, God or Thunder?

"May I sit with you a while, my son?" He walked around and got in without waiting for my answer. I might have said no. He didn't give me a chance.

I offered him some coffee. He declined. But he bummed a smoke. Too late to say I was out. He already saw the open package lying on the seat between us still half full. He helped himself. I pushed in the lighter beside the full ashtray, but he fumbled in his shirt pocket and produced a bright yellow Bic. Daffodil yellow, maybe it *was* Easter.

"There are few who seek the Lord today, my son. I am afraid that if he were to run for election, he would lose."

"Why do you say that?"

"Because it's true."

I think that Chaplain wanted to tell about the good things God has done, about salvation and all that. He just started off down the wrong track and, once he got going, well there was no holding him back.

"It's true. People haven't really turned their backs on God. It's God turned His back on the people."

I started to speak but he held up his hand and silenced me.

"The people are looking for wonder. Their spirits seek it — new age stuff, flying saucers, even going back to *your* religion. There is even a Sweatlodge in this place of penitence. People are trying to find God. But God has turned His back on the people. Now, maybe we deserve it, with all of our wars, greed, gluttony and lust. He is the Supreme Being, the Divine; only He can save the world. And He does nothing. Nothing, you hear. Nothing."

I shrugged and spread my hands palms up.

"No, there is no question. Why else are the murderers and rapists allowed to walk the Earth?" I looked toward the solid stone walls of Collins Bay Penitentiary.

"Why else do we hear of wars and rumours of wars? I know that's prophecy. But Rwanda, come on — and the Holocaust. How could He sit up there on His golden throne and witness that without lifting a finger? How?"

He rolled down his window and flicked an ash. The wind flowed through the cab, a spring wind from the South. It brought pleasantness and promise, I thought. He rolled his window back up. I left mine down.

"My son, you have come to a bankrupt Church. Faith has fled. Faith . . ." His face came to life at that word. "Faith is all there is. Faith in the supremacy of God — personal faith. I've carried it all my life. I was born with it . . . my parents, my parents. Now there was faith, and duty. My parents were staunch Catholics. I was raised in a God-fearing house. I was born in the Faith, and I have walked with faith all my life. It has sustained me and carried me. It has lifted me up and been my crutch. Faith has also been my sword and my armour. I have smote mine enemies with it."

I looked toward him at that. I had been watching the sun melt that bit of snow and ice that had been stuck under the windshield wipers all winter.

"But in the end, it is not enough. I need to see the hand of God."

I looked past Father Theodore at the giant tree that I did not recognize, the one that might be an Oak. Was it a relative if I didn't know it? I imagined the sap would be running now. There were tiny buds on the branches. It must be close to Easter. I could almost smell baked ham. Christians eat good once in a while — scalloped potatoes with a thick sauce burned to the pan, green beans from a can . . .

Father Theodore looked toward the maybe Oak. "Your people worship trees. Perhaps that's just as good. Trees don't answer either."

I thought about that. Crunched a Cheezie, offered the bag to the sad Father. He declined with a slow wave of his hand. The ash from his cigarette fell on the seat. Do we worship trees? I'd heard this stuff before. I waited. Father Theodore butted his smoke in the already full ashtray.

"Faith, my son. Pure faith, that's what we need to get us through." He reached over and patted my arm.

I watched as he slowly, steadily walked back to gate, placed a hand on the shoulder of the guard for a long second before he disappeared inside. The guard glared at me. It gave me a cold chill.

"Kingston is a weird place," I thought, as Thunder pulled back out onto the 401 and sped toward Toronto. Do we worship trees? Our relatives? Do we worship relatives? The key was the word *worship* — warship — friendship — kinship . . .

You know, I never ran away. That was not what I was up to when I walked out to the road and started to hitch-hike. That morning I snuck up on a mallard and shot it with a slingshot. One good round rock about the size of the end of my thumb — stretched rubber and smack — duck soup. I plucked that duck as best I could for a twelve-year-old and took it home for my mother to make soup. She wasn't home, so I left it on the counter where she would find it. It felt good to be a hunter, a provider. I think if I had missed that duck then my life would have been different. But, I hit it, first shot, head shot.

I think it was because I felt so good, so powerful or something, that I went out looking for something more. La Ronge did not have much, not back then, not things for a half-breed boy to do. A slingshot could be a good thing. It could also get a boy into trouble. Glass makes such a wonderful sound when a rock makes it tinkle. But I wasn't in trouble, not that day. That day I was a success, a boy wonder, a comic book hero, Slingshot Man.

The man who gave me a ride did not ask any questions. Just talked about selling stuff. He talked all the way to my grandfather's road where I asked to be let out. Nobody asked me any questions. Grandpa and Grandma were not even surprised to see me. She made sure I was fed and went back to working on the Moose hide that was starting to turn green and smell. I hung around there for a while, then borrowed my grandpa's fishing rod and walked down to the dock to try a few casts.

My grandpa was not a talker. I don't remember him ever using more than about three words at a time and sometimes those three words were a week apart. That was about how long it took for my mom to come find me. Mom could talk, she talked a lot, maybe to make up for her parents. She asked me why I ran away. What could I say? It was easier to say, "Because I don't like it there," than to explain about a duck and how it was when you shot something, and you needed something more but did not know what the more was.

Mom, Grandma, and Grandpa sat on the veranda of the old house, the one that burned down, and I fished. They talked a long while and I kept fishing. Cast out to where the weeds began, tried to lure that big Jack out, the one that ate all my grandpa's hooks before the fall. The sun danced on the water, sparkles of brilliance. The wind teased the Earth and everything that day was about play. Birds, and frogs, and fish, and water, and wind, and me, and the sunshine, and cast, and reel, and hope, and cast, and reel. I thought I would have to go home and only wanted to catch that big bugger before I left.

But, I didn't have to go home. I *was* home. Mom came down to the dock after about a thousand casts, well maybe only a hundred. My grandpa did not like me to exaggerate, I would learn. Mom put her arms around me, hugged me real tight, too tight to hug a twelve-year-old. I started to squirm and she held me by the shoulders at arm's length and looked into my eyes. I figured it was important so I looked back into hers. Her eyes were bright that sunshiny afternoon. I could see myself in the dark brown, so that's what I looked at.

"My boy, remember that you can come home anytime that you want." I figured she meant in about a week or so and that was okay with me. "Your Grandpa and Grandma are getting old and they want you to stay and help them out." I nodded. I understood this part, Grandpa could split wood, make that old axe do miracles on a knotty block of pine, but he had trouble bending over. He took a real long time to get an arm load. "You be good now, you hear me. I don't want to hear that you got into any mischief out here. Your Grandparents don't need any of your tricks." I nodded again, but I was trying to think of what tricks she was talking about. She hugged me close again and I let her, and didn't squirm until it was just too hard to stand still anymore.

That's how I came to live with Grandpa and Grandma. When fall came, I figured I would have to go to school and started to worry because there was no school close. Maybe I would have to go home. But the leaves changed, and me and Grandpa cut firewood. Cord after cord of dry pine piled into Grandpa's old Chev panel truck. Thirteen cords that fall and every fall after. Grandpa figured a cord a month and one more for good measure.

Grandma picked cranberries. Pail after pail of dark red tiny berries. She sat on the thick green moss and smiled when I came by. It didn't seem like she was even working and the pails filled up. She carried a mason jar filled with tea and a handkerchief wrapped around a soft piece of fresh bannock with lard and jam. The pails filled up and I carried them back to the house. Grandma showed me how to take the berries down to the lake where there was more wind and slowly pour the berries from the pail into a cardboard box. The wind seemed to know when we needed its help and gladly blew the leaves and little sticks away while I poured.

That fall I helped Grandma because she told me to. I didn't know yet about stewed cranberries and pancakes and thick golden syrup on cold winter mornings. The next fall I was on the ground beside her filling the pails and my face.

Early winter was about trapping. Walking behind Grandpa and setting traps for Fisher, Martin, Mink and Foxes. In the house at night with a cup of tea with Grandma, I watched Grandpa skin and stretch. "*Cheestee*," he would say, "check it out," and I would go over and he would show me something. Maybe how to conceal a cut in the hide by shaving a piece of skin from somewhere else and pasting it over the hole where it would dry and the Hudson's Bay Store manager would never notice. Grandpa never explained what he was doing. Just "*Cheestee*," and I would watch whatever he wanted to show me.

I pulled over at Trenton. I figured, "Why eat Cheezies when you have pockets full of money." I found a promising looking restaurant and pulled Thunder into the parking lot. A well-dressed Indian, and I mean well-dressed, and his wife were entering the restaurant at the same time. We stood together in front of the "Please wait to be seated" sign, the promise of good food. I nodded at him. The right thing to do to a man who is staring at you like you might be a relative or something. He nodded back. Maybe we *were* related or something. I stuck out my hand, fingers orange from eating Cheezies.

"Name's Charlie Muskrat."

"Bert Russel. Do I know you, Charlie?"

"Maybe." I wasn't sure.

"This is Erica." Bert indicated the brilliantly-dressed woman who was reading the specials board and trying not to stand too close to me. She turned at the sound of her name, looked me up and down and away without a nod. I had a flash at that moment. Sun-Dogs. Yeah, Sun-Dogs. Bright, brilliant flares from horizon to mid sky. One on either side of a winter sun. The promise of three more days of very cold weather.

"Where you from, Charlie?" Bert asked. Maybe he was trying to make up for his wife's chill with a little warm conversation.

"Out West." I put my grandmother's kindness into my voice to ease his little shame. That hint of kindness brought something out of Bert. I saw it in his face. In his Indian face.

"Oh, really. What brings you down East?"

"Just wandering around a bit, I guess."

"Well then, why don't you join us? I'm sure Erica won't mind." She turned and shrugged. Boredom was never so beautiful. She did not look at me again until I ordered a T-bone steak. I figured what the hell, I can afford it. I could feel the wads of money in my pockets. But the look on her face told me she suspected me of being a mooch, a big mooch.

"So what do you do for a living?"

"Oh, I trap a little and commercial fish when the season is open."

"Any money in that?

"Not a lot. Enough."

"I envy you." Bert sipped his coffee while we waited for the waitress to return with our food. "Sometimes I wish I had done more of that."

"He's becoming nostalgic again." Erica played with a spoon. Polished it with her napkin.

"It's not nostalgia. That's a word that goes back to the sixteen hundreds, June 22nd, 1652 to be exact, when a Swiss doctor came up with a word to describe the symptoms experienced by troops who were forced to be away from their homes and families."

She sighed and looked at her curved reflection in the spoon.

I was impressed. "How did you know that?"

"He thinks he knows everything."

We both ignored her, left her to her boredom.

"I've spent my life learning. When I was younger, I made sure that I would not end up like everyone else around me. I wanted more and I went out and got it."

"So what did you get?"

Bert wanted to brag and I opened the door for him.

"Let me tell you. When I was on the reservation, I saw quickly that the power was in the administration. The Indian agent was the real power. So I spent time watching him. I hung around and asked questions until he took me under his wing. I took whatever was offered and never looked back. I have three degrees and a portfolio that many men would envy. As I said, the power is in administration. An MBA opens doors, but once the door is open it is up to you to carry the action forward."

"He's always been the Indian that would." She looked at Bert like she was trying to see through his ears. Like there was nothing there.

"Hell, yeah," Bert didn't know she was looking through his head. "I've gone further, and I've gone faster. Administration opens doors and the money is behind the door marked *Imports*."

"Imports. Like what?"

"Like anything that is expensive. Don't waste time importing the cheap stuff; even if you do it in bulk, it is still cheap stuff. I mean, Cartier watches, Mercedes, Rolls, anything with a bit of class to it. Success is about doing business with style." Bert was on a roll. "A good product will sell itself, then you don't have to worry about placement. People. Well, when it comes to people, you cut out as many as you can between production and purchase. Don't try to be too big. Big is expensive, and success has to be shared. Of course there is always the element of luck."

I'm not sure if he paused for emphasis, and was going to tell me more or not. I had a sudden flash. "I know about luck. Good luck stones."

He opened his mouth but no words came out, so I kept talking. "Yeah, here." I pulled the little bag of stones out from under my shirt, slipped the leather thong over my head and there they were on the table between us, a little leather bag with the stones spilling out. "See, good luck stones."

"Holy shit! Erica would you look at this."

"What." She was still bored.

"Diamonds. Raw bloody diamonds," he was holding one of my good luck stones up to the light, not that there was much light in the restaurant.

"Let me see," she tried to snatch the stone from Bert.

He kept it from her. "This baby must be a dozen carats if it's anything." He turned away from her and held it up to the light again. He closed one eye, but just for a second, then he opened it again and watched Erica.

I felt something at my crotch. It was Erica's foot, nylon encased toes. She faced Bert, her eyes toward me. I looked back, tried to see into those eyes behind the cat-eye glasses. It wasn't warmth that I saw there.

"Excuse me Mr. Muskrat." I turned to see a very shorthaired man in a blue suit standing at my shoulder.

"Yes."

"I am Ron Smith from the Department of Indian Affairs."

"I'm not having an affair." I looked toward Erica. She was leaning her head against Bert's shoulder and smiling all innocent and cute. Bert kept his left hand palm down on the table. I assumed the good luck stone was under it.

"Mr. Muskrat, I understand that you received an amount of money from the Federal Government. Pursuant to the *Indian Fiscal Accountability Act* it is my job to ensure that the entire two hundred and seventy-four dollars and twenty-five cents that you received are properly accounted for. Have you spent any of the funds you received?"

"Well, I put a couple of those quarters into a parking meter."

"Did you obtain a receipt?"

"Well, no."

"In the event that receipts are not obtainable, and I assume that you used a public meter instead of an authorized parking facility, you are required by section twelve thousand nine hundred and eighty-four, subsection eighteen 'G' of the regulations pursuant to that Act to fill out forms 'K', 'P' and 'V'."


WESAKICAK OPENED HIS EYES IN THE mist. Yawned, stretched and scratched his ass. The Muses were still debating.

"If Strauss was a painter, would his art move the world?"

"If Churchill spoke poetry, would the world have followed him to war?"

Wesakicak, checked the toe sticking through a hole in his moccasin. He scraped the crescent of black under the nail with a fingernail. The black was now under there. He scraped it with a thumbnail, now it was under there. Wesakicak looked around. No one was paying any attention to him. He scraped the thumbnail with the toenail, and pulled his moccasin over the dirt-encrusted digit.

"What you go and do that for?"

Wesakicak looked around to see who was talking to him. The man with one arm was talking to the man wearing shredded clothes that smelled of exploded dynamite, a cordite stink around him. He stuck a finger in his ear and wriggled it around. "What?" he asked as he cleaned out the other ear. "What a blast."

"Asshole!" The other man picked up his arm and stuck it back on.

"What you go and do that for?" asked a young woman looking around for her parcels. She pushed a dress back into its torn paper wrapping. "I was looking forward to wearing that." The dress fell out the other side of the package. "Oh well, I suppose I should be happy. I always thought you couldn't bring it with you."

Cordite Man looked around at the crowd that was gathering, forming in the mist. "Six, seven, eight." He counted with a pointing finger.

"What you go and do that for?"

"What you go and do that for?" they asked as they emerged.

"To go to heaven," answered Cordite Man, as he removed the wide leather belt with the bits of wire and the leftovers of exploded dynamite. He dropped the belt and never looked at it again.

"Well, here we are," said the man as he flexed his arm, good as new.

"What are you guys doing here?" asked Cordite Man.

"Same as you, idiot, come to heaven," said the old lady with the glass shard in her face and a hole in her chest. She looked around, got her bearings and started off toward the high, white wall with the shiny gate. Cordite Man followed her as did the young lady, and the man with two arms, and the rest. Wesakicak fell into line behind them.

"Rosella Stienne," said the old lady to the man in the white robe with the big book. He ran his finger down the page.

"Not today," he said.

"Do I look like I'm supposed to be here today?" snapped the old lady. "Try a little further ahead."

Peter flipped pages, found her name and stroked it off with a quill.

"Next."

"Gloria Phyplia, You'll have to look a long ways ahead to find me."

"George Nexar."

"Erin Moore."

"Cassandra Laura Robinson."

Peter flipped pages, stroked names and waved each through the gate.

"Mustafa Goldstein," Cordite man stated proudly.

Peter flipped pages, stopped, started over, flipped more pages, looked up. "Sorry, Mustafa, your name isn't in the book."

Mustafa's once proud face fell. "How can that be?" Tears formed in the corners of his eyes.

"I am teasing you, my friend." Peter let out a little chuckle, some days are pure fun. "You're in here." He stroked out an entry and waved Mustafa in.

"How about Charlie Muskrat?" Wesakicak asked.

Peter checked the book, forward, forward some more. "Not here, Wesakicak."

"You know me?"

"Yes, Wesakicak, everyone knows about you. When we took the stories about you away from the Indians, we brought them up here. You're one of the favourites in the big library."

"Is that a fact? You're not trying to tease me now, are you?"

"I would never tease anyone who was older than myself. Especially not you, Wesakicak." Peter closed the book and rested his elbows on it. "So, my friend, why are we concerned with this Charlie Muskrat?"

"Oh nothing, I was just curious."

"Is he on his way?"

"I hope not. I was just wondering where he would go."

"Probably down in the valley. Just follow the river until you come to a forest. Ask the people there."

Wesakicak felt like he was getting somewhere now, as he headed away from the gate.

Grandma made Grandpa build a partition at the back of the cabin "so Charlie can have some privacy."

"I don't need privacy, Grandma."

"Young boys becoming men need privacy."

I knew better than to argue with Grandma when she took that tone. Grandpa knew better than me. He never said a word. He just went out, cut a few trees, peeled them for supports, hammered them into place, and built a wall. I didn't need half of the back of the cabin for myself, but that's what I got. My cot in the corner took no space at all. The bare plank floor of the rest of my private space seemed way to big. Grandma cut a large cardboard rectangle that lay on the floor by my bed. In the morning when I swung my feet out from under the covers, it really wasn't any warmer than the bare wood. But Grandma had made it for me, so I tried to keep it clean and put it back when it slid by itself under the bed.

Late winter, early spring was about catching shorthaired fur: Muskrat, Beaver, and Otter. That was the best, or close to the best time of the year. Early spring, when the sun has heat to it again, and the snow is turning a little slushy, and the Muskrat houses are starting to show through the deep winter snow, and Grandpa and me setting traps, and you don't have to wear a toque or even mitts, man, that was the life. When we got home with a pack sack full of Muskrat, Grandma would skin them, put them out on the smoke rack for a few hours over a slow fire of green poplar, then roast them in the white enamel wood-fired cook stove. After a day of walking in spring air that you can breathe deep again without freezing your lungs, the smell of a roasting Muskrat would just about drive me crazy with hunger, especially if Grandma had a fresh-baked bannock on the sideboard wrapped in a clean dish towel to keep it moist.

"It won't be long, my boy. Bring in some firewood while you wait. I need some chopped small for the cook stove."

"Can I have a piece of bannock and jam first?"

"If you want. But it might be better to wait."

Grandma knew best. I'd wait. Then with my belly full and the sun just below the horizon, I inevitably found my cot with the Rabbit robe cover, and sleep would find me fast. You don't see Rabbit robes anymore. Grandma used a quilt on one side and a flannel sheet on the other. In between these, she sewed a liner made from woven strips of Rabbit fur. Forget down-filled. Ducks don't winter well. If you really want to sleep warm in a Canadian winter, you want to sleep under a Rabbit robe. If you are stuffed with Muskrat and bannock and fresh tea and the cabin is warm, you won't even mind if your pillow is a sweater folded so the zipper is on the inside. Sleep will rise up from that cot and inhale you.

Sometimes I would wake up and listen to the night. At night, on a trap line, there is nothing to listen to. It is silent, absolute black, and silent. Even with the wall I could hear Grandma and Grandpa's breathing, my own heart, thump, thumping softly under the Rabbit robe. Sometimes I would hear "Wally" the

Weasel scurrying around in the dark. Grandma encouraged him with bits of meat. He never became a pet. You never pet a Weasel, but with a Weasel in a cabin you never have to worry about mice.

Sometimes I heard other things.

"Uh, Uh, Uh, Uh,"

"Shh, old man,"

"What? You want it faster?"

"Shhh, you'll wake the boy."

"What? Harder?"

"Shhhh! The boy"

"You want it where?"

"SHHHHHH!"

"Better be quiet, old woman, you'll wake the boy."

Ron Smith of the Department of Indian Transgressions packed me away from that restaurant with Bert and Erica. I had a stack of forms beside me on the seat of Thunder as I headed up the 401 toward Toronto.

"Should've just given the money back," I confided to Thunder. But Ron never gave me much of a chance. He dominated all conversation from the moment of his appearance at my shoulder until I promised that I would fill out every one of those damn forms in triplicate and report all expenditures and swear an oath not to spend a penny on trivialities.

Late at night on the 401, the sky takes on a metallic hue. Strangest sky I have ever seen. No stars, no moon. It is like the Northern Lights died and someone spread their ashes across the heavens. Like being inside a cook pot with a domed enamel lid the firelight seeps through. How can a person tell direction in a place like this?

I don't remember the sky the first time I came to Toronto. That bus ride must have been at least thirty years ago. My seventeen-year-old eyes were too wide open to see much.

Grandma cooked all that late August day. Something was coming for me. I knew, with each cast off the old dock. The big Jackfish played with me, stealing hooks, and even broke water once so that I could get a good look at him. His long body, behind a head of teeth, curled and waved a wide tail before it disappeared back into the lake.

Grandpa came down to the dock to get me with a slight beckoning wave. I reeled in the dangling hook, put the rod into the canoe out of the way and followed him up to the cabin. My mother, my brother James, Aunt Annie and a couple of cousins had arrived. A big square tarpaulin spread on the ground held a large pot of soup, bowls of bannock, Fish, Moose meat, potatoes and carrots.

"Serve your relatives," Grandpa led me to the edge of the tarpaulin.

When the meal was over, when everyone was fed and an offering of a little of each food was set aside for the ancestors, Grandpa came and stood behind me.

"Stand up, my boy."

I stood and looked around. Everyone smiled and sat up straighter. Grandpa took me by the shoulders and turned me to the West. Everyone turned with me. Grandpa sang a song, turned me to the North and sang again. Then to the East and South; everyone turned with us. When the song was done Grandpa leaned close and whispered the Indian name that was for me to use to help me through my life.

Then Grandpa told me to hand out the gifts. There were moccasins that smelled of the smoke of Grandma's tanning, blankets from the Hudson's Bay Store, and softened Beaver pelts in perfect ovals. Grandpa would hand me a gift, tell me who it was for, and I would give the gift to that person, shake his or her hand, and return to Grandpa for the next gift. The Hudson's Bay blanket was for my mother. I could feel her emotion as she ignored my offered hand and, instead, stood and gave me a long hug.

When the pile of gifts was all handed out, the leftover food put into containers for people to take home with them, and the tarp shook out and folded away, everyone walked with me to the highway. Just before the bus arrived, Grandpa gave me the ticket for Toronto. Toronto was about as far as Grandpa and Grandma could imagine from northern Saskatchewan.

"You are a man now, with a man's name. It is time for you to go out into the world." Grandpa did not need to say more.

"You are a good boy, remember that. I mean you are a good man, or you will be a good man." Grandma was having trouble with this. Instead of words she decided to give me a long hug that I can still remember. I can still remember my mother's hug, too, as we stood on the edge of the gravel road, and I felt the pull of the open bus door behind me, tugging at me, impatient for me to go.

I remember that first time coming into Toronto. I was too young to feel lonely. The excitement overrode everything else. There was still feast food in my pack sack and money in my pocket. I was seventeen, alive and ready. Toronto was the beginning of an adventure.

Four lanes flow into six lanes and flow into twelve lanes and I am a fish in spawn on a fast black river, and Thunder doesn't know which way to go so he just goes. The black river glimmers and flashes between smears of windshield wipers. Slush and salt smatter the glass and I think I must be a Salmon to be swimming in salt water.

WESAKICAK TOOK A SHORTCUT ACROSS THE grassy place toward a row of trees that indicated where a river should flow down into the valley.

"Fore," someone shouted and a little white ball dropped beside him and rolled down the slope into a gold cup. "What the . . . ?" Wesakicak looked around. A group of men and women stood up the slope from him. "May we play through, Brother?" one of the men asked.

"Doesn't matter to me, as long as this isn't Oka." Wesakicak continued on his way. It really didn't matter.

Another man placed a little white ball on a silver spike and whacked it into the air. It curved toward the row of trees that Wesakicak had been headed toward. A dove of brilliant white flew out of the trees, grabbed the ball out of the air and carried it over the patch of carpet grass. It let the ball drop up the slope from the golden cup. The ball rolled gently across the uniform, jade-green grass. The perfect blades of grass bent before the ball and oozed it toward the hole.

"A hole in one!" shouted the man, his golf club above his head in both hands.

"Again," said a woman.

"Of course," said the next golfer as he placed a little white ball on a silver spike.

Wesakicak walked toward the row of trees, ducked through the eucalyptus, and followed the slight trail down toward the sliver of blue that reflected puffy white clouds against a sky of deeper blue.

The river water flowed clean and cool between grassy banks. As Wesakicak followed it along away from Heaven, the grass gradually changed from a uniform carpet to taller, thicker blades. The river flowed into a forest. Wesakicak stopped and looked around when he entered it. The trees brought back a distant memory.

"I haven't seen this since Creation."

Everything was new. The trees were the original trees. The dewdrops on the leaves were the first ever to rest on green life. The sunlight that sparkled on the dew was the first light, the light that began Creation. The Deer that watched Wesakicak through large, clear, bright eyes was First Deer.

"Hey, my Brother."

"Hello to you, Wesakicak."

"Where are we, my Brother?"

Deer looked around. His head moved with grace at the end of his long neck.

"Here," he answered.

"But, where is here?"

The question had no meaning to Deer. He nibbled a bit of sweet grass, let the clump roll in his mouth for a moment. When the juice of the grass filled and washed all of his taste buds, Deer swallowed, looked back at Wesakicak, and shrugged the way only a Deer with sweet grass juice in its mouth can shrug.

Deer looked delicious. Wesakicak heard his stomach rumble. Venison roast, barbequed ribs, just look at those long slender legs, soup bones. Sunlight slanted through the trees and painted Deer in splotches. Where the light struck him, his coat showed the shine of good health. Wesakicak imagined the layer of fat that must lie just beneath that coat, a trim of white on the edge of a steak, stew meat simmering in a pot. Oh yeah, and tongue, and kidneys, and liver, and marrow . . .

"You'll never change, will you, Wesakicak?" Long slender legs lifted Deer in a bound that carried him into the trees and away.

A dribble of drool found its way to Wesakicak's chin. He wiped it away and followed Deer deeper into the forest.

The wonderful smell of wood smoke and roasting meat drew Wesakicak away from Deer's tracks. No need to track down food when someone was cooking. Wesakicak followed his nose to a clearing.

"Hie, Wesakicak. Come eat with us."

The camp was small. Two wigwams of white birch-bark, their doors open to the sunlight, stood at the back of the opening in the trees. The forest canopy overhead yawned to let the sun brighten the grassy expanse of the camp. The man stood at his place on the ground beside the wigwam's door and beckoned Wesakicak into the camp with big generous arm motions.

"Come, Wesakicak, come and share our food." He murmured something to the woman beside him.

"It would be nice to hear from our relatives," she agreed as she added another stick to the fire.

"Come, Wesakicak. Our great-great-granddaughter had a feast and remembered us. There's roast Deer meat, and soup and berries and bannock and cookies and tea enough for all of us."

Wesakicak feigned shyness as he walked slowly into the camp, head down. His hunger urged him to rush the food but propriety demanded that he be patient.

"Sit here, the grass is soft and warm." The jubilant man indicated a spot beside him. The woman brought Wesakicak a birch-bark plate, its edges curled up. A Deer rib heavy with meat and fat protruded from both sides of the bark. A huge piece of buttered bannock nearly toppled from the pile of food. Wesakicak's stomach rumbled ever so softly.

"Our great-great-granddaughter had a feast and remembered us." The man repeated proudly.

"She is a good child." Wesakicak talked around the Deer rib. "How old is she?"

"Oh, she must be nearly eighty," answered the woman. "She'll be here soon, we expect."

"Eat lots now," said the man. "After she comes, I doubt we will eat this good for a long time."

"Why's that?"

"There's no one behind her who remembers."

Wesakicak finished sucking the very last bit of meat from the Deer rib. The bone, completely bare, looked sun bleached. He held it in his hand as he talked, waved it in the air for emphasis. "I know what you mean. The last food I had was a handful of Cheezies from Charlie Muskrat. Do you know Charlie Muskrat? He's a good guy. Tries hard."

The man looked at the woman. They both shook their heads. "Not one of our relatives," answered the woman. "We're related to the Kiseyinew people. Do you know any Muskrat people?" she asked her husband.

"Muskrats. Didn't there used to be Muskrats over by Thunder Mountain that way? Seems to me there were some."

"Those are the ones." Wesakicak licked the berry juice from the Birch bark. "Are there any relatives around here?"

"Over towards the river are some people who might know. Here, give me your plate and I will refill it. There's plenty."

Wesakicak ate another plate, and another plate, then had a little sleep. When he awoke two days later the camp had another visitor. A blond man in long, white robes sat cross legged, his back to a tree, and drank from an earthen jug.

"You're awake." The man offered the jug.

"I know you from somewhere, but I can't quite place it." Wesakicak took the jug and drank. He spat it out. "That's wine!"

"Thou should not waste," the old hippie took back the jug. "I say onto you, I have always liked it here in the wilderness. Here there is peace," he brushed a strand of long blond hair aside and took a swig from the jug. He continued sadly, "That gold and silver place beyond is far too cosmopolitan for me. Sometimes I do think the people who come there would be happier in Disneyland."

"Times change." Wesakicak was beginning to understand the sorrow in this man.

"They do," the man took another swig from the jug, set it on his knee a moment and changed his mind. He lifted the jug again and this time glugged loudly as he poured it opulently down his throat. "I suppose it does not much matter that the newly arrived are short of grace. Live and let live, that is what I have always said. So, I let them their pleasant pastimes. At least here in the wilderness a man can hear himself think." He passed the jug to Wesakicak.

The wine did not belong here, but it was offered in friendship. Wesakicak touched the bulging bottle to his lips and let a little seep into his mouth. He wished he had something to rinse with after his drink. Why would anyone want berry juice that had gone bad? He made a face.

"Did you not enjoy it? I made it from river water." He leaned forward as he reached out for the jug, and almost fell away from the tree. He caught his balance and the heavy earthen vessel at the same time, and leaned back. "I was trying for a nice rich red, perhaps you would prefer a white or a rose," he slurred.

"I'm not much for wine. Prefer water or cherry juice."

"As ye desire, so shall ye have, or have not. If ye do not partake of the wine, then there is more for me," he glugged the jug again. "The day cometh when I shall return. And on that day I must set aside my jug and take up a gavel instead. On that day, both joyous and cruel, I might find pity for those like me, those of the wilderness who remember what peace there is in silence."

"What do you know about Charlie Muskrat?" Wesakicak was concerned.

"Charlie Muskrat?" Jesus thought a moment. "Charlie Muskrat." He scratched at the bit of beard on his chin. "I do not know Charlie Muskrat. Does he know me?"

"Sometimes he sings old songs to you."

"I will listen for him." Jesus leaned his head back against the tree.

Wesakicak stood, stretched himself to his full height. "Well, I gotta be goin'." He nodded toward Jesus and walked away, thinking about a drink of clean water from the river.

Jesus closed his eyes and drifted away on a cloud of red wine.


THE RAIN WAS JUST TOO HEAVY to keep going so I pulled over to have a sleep. I figured I was tired enough that I could sleep through the noise of the 401. The trucks slogging through the night churning salt and slush were no bother. It was the sirens that screamed up my backbone and kept me twisting in my sleep. Mary gently pushed me awake. I rolled over and looked into her eyes. She lay beside me in the loft bed, her head resting on her hand, her elbow on the pillow. "You had me worried, Charlie." The hand on her cheek muffled her voice.

"How's that?"

"You've never been away this long before. I was beginning to wonder if you were coming home."

"Soon as I'm done, my love."

"Soon as you're done what?"

My hand found the roundness of her hip under the covers. My fingers wanted to play there awhile.

"Soon as you're done what?" She leaned closer. Her face bathed in moonlight smiled slightly, but there was worry around the eyes.

"Soon as I'm done, my love."

"Come on, Buddy. Time to wake up. You can't sleep here." The OPP officer pulled me by the foot.

I wanted to tell Mary everything was going to be okay, that I would be home again and it would be as before.

"What have we got?" The second officer spoke over the shoulder of the first as they both leaned in through Thunder's open door.

"Looks like someone maybe had a little too much to drink and couldn't make it home. Come on, Buddy, rise and shine. Time to go sit in the nice police car."

The back seat of the car was made of hard plastic. Kind of like how the seats used to be in a McDonald's except these were moulded into the floor. The safety glass partition opened and the passenger side officer turned toward me. "I need you to blow into this machine again."

I blew into the nozzle again, and again the light stayed green. The officer scratched his head. "How much did you have to drink tonight?" He shook the machine. The light did not change.

"Like your machine said, nothing."

"So what were you doing sleeping on the side of the highway."

"Sleeping."

I followed the officer's advice when he gave me back my licence and registration. I turned off the 401 at the next exit and headed North until I found a quiet back road and rolled up in the sleeping bag again.

*My dad was there when they signed the Treaties. He refused to sign. Said he didn't want to live on a Reserve."* Grandma's story replayed, probably triggered by the demand for my driver's licence. I wanted to think about the dream and Mary, but Grandma kept telling her story. *That old man wanted to live the way he always had, free to go wherever he wanted, whenever he wanted and he did. He said the government had no right to make us buy a hunting licence, or a fishing licence. Said that was made clear to them at the Treaty. To the day he died, he refused to buy a licence. Said the day would come when an Indian would need a licence to go* misi *in the bush. My brothers used to buy the hunting and fishing licences for him, but the old man wouldn't even carry them, so the boys kept them for him.*

"Thanks, Grandma, I'll remember that." I pulled the sleeping bag over my head for the darkness. Even out here in the country, miles away from Toronto, the night is polluted with light. I looked again for Mary but her image refused to appear.

I felt people watching me as I let my feet find their way down Bay Street. It wasn't their fault, really. After all, it is not everyday that a man wearing a Beaver jacket and hat comes to Toronto. The city, in that moment, felt like a very small town where the curious stare. The people who looked quickly away when I met their gaze, would themselves be the subject of scrutiny if they were to walk down La Ronge Avenue, all looking exactly the same in their dark blue suits. Clones, I thought with a shudder. Were these people genetically identical? They certainly looked it. Not just the suits and ties. Every one of them had the same haircut, the same cup of Starbuck's coffee, and the same shoes.

I heard a voice. "Hi, Charlie." A woman's voice.

I looked around. There was no one close to me. There were people on the street, walking, looking away, looking straight ahead and walking faster.

Then there was a hand on my shoulder, a gentle hand. "It's all right, Charlie."

"Who are you?" I still could not see anyone.

"It's me. Paulette, your sister."

"How come I can't see you?"

"I disappeared."

"I don't get it." A man stared straight into my face as he walked by, flipped a loonie at me, and kept going without breaking stride. I caught the coin, felt the cold of it in my palm. Paulette was laughing.

"Careful who you talk to, Charlie. People might think something is the matter with you."

I still didn't get it. I felt around in front of me.

"Right here." A warm hand found mine, a gentle hand. It squeezed lightly. "I'm still in your world, just invisible."

"What happened to you?"

"I don't know. One day I was there walking to the university and the next thing I knew, I disappeared."

"Can you come back?"

"I hope so. It's the shits to be disappeared. But I don't think there is anything you can do, Charlie. I just wanted to say hello."

"Hello."

I heard Paulette laugh again. "You take care, Charlie, and don't be talking to strangers." The little hand slipped out of mine. I felt the peck of a kiss on my cheek. "There's lots and lots of us, Charlie, all over the place. Did you know that anywhere else in the world if people begin to disappear and the police don't do anything, the people begin to suspect the police for the disappearances." Then she was gone. I stood there listening to the sound of Paulette's squishy running shoes becoming fainter.

My felt-lined boots suddenly felt much too warm against the bare pavement. They were the perfect choice when I started out a few days ago. But today in Toronto I felt like I was in another country, a much warmer country. The snowdrifts and whiteness of my homeland were replaced with dry concrete and dust.

The spring sun found its way through the thick, city sky. In its attempt to bring life to this place, it heated the cement, steel and glass. Here the only green is painted on signs or awnings and of course every Starbuck's shop. With nothing to absorb the sun's gift, the heat was reflected, rejected. The beaver jacket that Mary made for me was much too warm.

That was her name, wasn't it. Mary. I remembered Mary's name. I repeated it. Mary, Mary. Why would I remember it here? There was nothing here that spoke of her. This was all noise and confusion. Mary was peace and quiet. There was only the jacket that gently hugged me.

Head down, I followed my feet as the concrete flowed under me. Up Bay Street, a left to Spadina, then up the slope again. I was looking for something, a memory, a pre-Mary memory. I wasn't trying to push her from my mind, I was letting go. Letting Mary go. Distance and time without resistance and she would fade into the trees and mists of the North.

How long had I been leaving? Since the diamonds? Maybe. Earlier? I don't think so. There wasn't a point where I said, "I am going to leave." It wasn't like that. I just started to think about away more than home. When I stared into the distance, Mary would come and kiss me on the forehead. Look into my face. Read me. Then go back to her sewing, or reading, or whatever. I didn't plan to come to Toronto. Thunder brought me here. I let it happen.

THE MOSS UNDER WESAKICAK'S FEET FELT soft through the holes in his moccasins. Sunlight splattered the ground through the high boughs and changed the colour of the moss from dark green, to bright jade, to polished emerald. Wesakicak watched Raven dance from one foot to another around the food left on a large, raised, flat rock.

"What have you got there, my Brother?"

"An offering. And it's for me. Not for you, Wesakicak."

"I wasn't trying to get it from you."

"I know you better than that." Raven straddled the small birch-bark plate covered with bits of meat. On guard.

Wesakicak sat down in the moss, felt the comfort of it on his behind. Patience. "Do you know the relatives of Charlie Muskrat?"

"Why?"

"Why what?"

"Why do you want to know about Charlie's relatives?" Raven looked to his food, gobbled a piece quickly, and looked back up to watch Wesakicak.

"Well, Charlie seems to have become a pet project of mine."

"What's in it for you?"

"Nothing."

"Nothing?"

"Nothing, honest"

"Honest? Somehow honest and Wesakicak don't seem to go together."

"I've changed. It's not like it used to be, my Brother. Times have changed."

"Sure they have." Raven quickly gobbled another piece of meat. Three pieces left. "Okay, I'll play along. Charlie's relations camp at the river forks most of the time. They have a meadow where wild onions and celery grow together. In one branch of the river they catch Pike, and in the other they catch Trout." Raven choked down another piece.

Wesakicak noted that the meat looked tender and nicely roasted. "Who gave you the food?"

"Some people still remember me. Don't you get offerings?" Raven raised an eyebrow. It made his face lopsided. "I thought you wanted to know about Charlie's relatives?"

"I do, I do. I was just curious about the meat."

"Yeah, right." Raven grabbed one, then the other piece, spread his wings and lifted off and away.


I FOUND THE PLACE I WAS looking for, the Silver Dollar. I went into the dark where the smell of old beer, the twang of a guitar and a moaning harmonica awaited me. I stood, letting my eyes adjust a moment, then found the pool tables off to the side. Memory drew me there and I followed that memory to the green velvet and dark wood and the clash and flash and fall of red and black balls.

"Charlie Muskrat! Hey you, get over here." The voice came from a shadow man in black standing by the far table. He laid his cue on the table without care, ticking a red ball out of position. A man opposite raised his hands, palms up, in a "what the fuck" sign. The man in the black shirt and black leather vest waved him off. "Come back tomorrow and I'll take your money." Then he was around the table, the all-white smile, teeth in perfect order, arms stretched wide. He swept toward me and grabbed me in a huge hug. "Man, Charlie, what the hell are you doing here? I was quite content to never, ever see you, and here you are sneaking into the Silver Dollar again." He released the hug and held me by the shoulders at arm's length to stare into my face.

"So?" the big smile asked, and it was my turn to speak, but I couldn't remember his name. The face was familiar. I should know the name that went with it — Gems? Rubies? Diamonds? My face must have shown puzzlement.

"Jules," he said. "You don't remember me." His face showed disappointment, "Maybe that's a good thing." And the white smile came back. Then I remembered, in a rush, hitchhiking to California, him taking care of me, a big brother who always wanted to know, "Have you eaten today, Charlie?", who didn't find his sleeping bag until he knew I was safe in mine, who wouldn't let me shoot pool, but always slipped me a few dollars from his wins.

"Why'd you come back?" Jules asked seriously. I really had no answer so I sipped the beer he bought for me and looked down at the table a moment, then back up to his face. "I don't know, the wind kinda pushed me this way."

"Don't matter." He slid his beer around in the wet, clinked a ring against the glass, a huge gold thing with a black J on its face. "This." He read my stare and held up the ring toward me. "A gift from a special lady. By the way, how's Mary?"

"Fine, I guess."

"Tell me everything is cool between you. Tell me Mary is safe at home waiting."

"Mary's good."

"And everything is good between you?"

"Everything is good."

"For sure?"

"For sure."

"So really now, what are you doing in Toronto again?"

How could I explain, I didn't know. I hadn't set out to come here. But I must have known somewhere in my thoughts, somewhere deep in there I must have known that I was coming here, I had just never let myself explore those thoughts. I had drifted here, and I had driven here, and here I was.

The Silver Dollar was the same and it wasn't. It was older and I was older, and Jules was seemingly much older than the bar and me. He had always been older than me, not much, a few years that wouldn't make a difference now, but was the biggest difference then. The eyes hadn't changed, they were the same. Eyes that had always been old, had always known more, and now they were on me, across the table, set in that solid face that was becoming more and more familiar as memory gave birth to memory:

*"Charlie, take Mary and go home. You don't belong here. You belong in the North with a trap line, and a cabin, or even just a tent. Here, take the money, go home. I want you to go home as much for me as for you. I need to know that there are real Indians somewhere living off the land and enjoying life, so that I can be an Indian in the city, so that somewhere in my mind I know that real Indians exist. You're that real Indian, Charlie. To me, you are the real Indian and I am the remains of an Indian. I need you to be in a real place while I am in this place. And if not me, Charlie, then think about Mary. You won't survive here, and she won't abandon you, so she won't survive here. Take Mary and go home, have a good life together, live the fairy tale, so that the rest of us can believe in something."*

I'd taken the money in one hand and Mary in the other, and went home. The money didn't make it all the way back, Mary did, and she was still there. But I was here, again, in the Silver Dollar and Jules' old eyes were asking why.

"Maybe I just came to see how you was."

"Naw, Charlie. I'm the con artist. I've had decades to practice my skill, that won't work. It's not just that I can spot a con from around the block. It's that you can't lie worth a damn, never could."

How do you answer a question that has no answer? There was no reason for me to be in Toronto. I knew that. I was just here. I fingered the leather pouch beneath my shirt, assured myself that the stones were real. If there was any reason for me to be in Toronto it was in that bag. Thirty-nine raw diamonds that I counted this morning, each a story or at least a chapter in a story that hadn't happened yet, a story that I would create, and walk in, a story different from the story of Mary and me.

Tomorrow I will sell the first diamond and begin the first chapter. Maybe some new clothes, a jet-black shirt and leather vest, like Jules', or maybe a blue suit and brown leather shoes without laces, and drink coffee from a paper cup on Bay Street. Maybe a haircut, shear the braids . . . The imagined tomorrow stalled there. Would I really cut my hair, cut it without being in mourning? If I indulged in the symbol of grief, would that bring grief? In this new story I would have to put away those old ideas. In the new story Indians don't have braids; they walk shoulder to shoulder with politicians and business folk, and go out for supper, or take a lunch and a glass of wine. They only wear buckskins when they go to the pow-wow at the Sky Dome, or is it the Rogers Centre now? Doesn't matter. I will walk with them through the turnstiles, pay my fee, and sit in the bleachers and watch the performance of Indians in regalia, and be thankful for central heating. The calluses on my hands from chopping wood will soften and I will be able to shake hands with the performers and they will know that my hands are the hands of a successful Indian.

"You can't do that, Charlie!"

I came out of my imagined tomorrow to find Harold Johnson sitting at our table.

"What can't I do?"

"You can't stay here."

"That's what I've been trying to tell him," Jules put in.

"What is this?" I looked back and forth at the two faces that both looked at me. Serious, determined, concerned, faces that forced me back into my chair. One the face of an old friend that I had just reunited with, had a history with; the other, a face I knew but I couldn't say I knew well. "What is this?" I asked again.

"Well, how do I explain?" Harold stumbled for words, his mouth moved on emptiness. He scratched his head. He looked to Jules for help, but Jules was leaning back waiting for the answer. "Well, Charlie, I know this is going to be a shock, but I created you. I set you out to find yourself and to have a bit of fun. Of course, I guess I sort of imagined a Cervantes kind of story but, instead of a steed named Rocinante, I gave you Thunder."

"Charlie as Don Quixote. That's good. I can see it, almost." Jules chuckled. "Who's your friend, Charlie?"

"Someone from back home. Writes stories and such. I think he's been too long with his nose between the pages, beginning to lose touch with reality."

"I know this will be hard for you. But you have to believe me. I wrote you, set you out as a bit of comedy but also as a satirical commentary on the social situation we find ourselves in today. You've been here in Toronto for months now."

"For months? Harold, I just saw you a few days ago. I just got here."

"Naw, you've been stuck here for months; writer's block they call it. Anyway my wife has been on me: 'What's happening with Charlie', 'You have to get Charlie out of Toronto'. She cares about you. I had to do something, see. I couldn't leave you here. Somehow it just wasn't right so I talked to my editor about coming here."

I played along; Harold was obviously very serious, poor guy. But just because someone is losing it, is no reason to be disrespectful. "And what did your editor say?"

"Oh, he cringed, turned away, twisted away. 'Post-modernism' he said with a shudder. But I had to do it. I can work it out with him later."

"Bring this man a drink." Jules waved at the waitress.

"No, its okay. I don't drink." Then to the waitress. "Maybe a ginger ale, please." He was struggling, having a hard time with whatever he needed to do for whatever reason he needed to do it. Jules was leaning forward now, sliding the Coors back and forth between both hands in the wet of the table, a little eager, a little entertained. I caught his eye and cautioned him to be kind. Jules can be brutal at times.

"Okay, Harold, I'll play along. If I am a character in one of your stories, what's in the little leather bag?"

"Diamonds."

I sat back. Jules' face froze in a half-amused smile. He wouldn't expose anything he didn't have to. I saw the deliberateness as he unfroze, sat back and sipped the Coors. The situation called for something; he chose amusement. "Diamonds? Charlie?" he nearly giggled.

Okay, so Harold guessed. Maybe he held some extra sight common to the special people, like the ones that I saw today walking the streets mumbling to themselves. I had to be careful not to injure him. "And where did I get them from?"

"I don't know. I haven't written that part yet."

Then it was clear. If Harold were rational he would have to see it also. He couldn't be my creator and not know where the diamonds came from. Poor guy.

"Listen, Harold, it'll be all right. If you need a hand, I'll buy you a bus ticket tomorrow. Go home and get some rest. You've had a rough winter."

"Let him hang around, Charlie, he's got the most original line I've ever heard."

There were a couple of ways this could go. Maybe Harold was one of those special people, those mumbling street people, partly in this world, partly in that other world, able to see things, or hear things, or feel things, whatever. Grandma always made sure that I was extra kind to people like that. *You don't have to believe what they say, but you have to respect their saying it. Listen closely, there might be a message in there for you.*

Maybe this was his idea of a practical joke and he was going to break into a smile and laugh soon. But, looking at him, unless he was a far better actor than I knew, his face said that he was more than serious. This was important to him.

In a way he was right. This was the wrong situation. But Harold had it wrong, backwards. It was he who shouldn't be here. He should be back in the North, with his dog team and trap line, living the life of the writer on the edge of the world, looking to the world from his isolation and writing from that pure perspective. He didn't belong here in a downtown bar. But then, maybe Harold was a contrary. One of those backward people that can see better than the rest of us because in actuality it is us who are going backwards.

"Hey, Harold. Tell us about Wesakicak." I tested my theory and maybe could move him away from this idea that he was the creator. Wesakicak, the trickster was the first contrary and creator. Want to pacify a storyteller, ask him to tell a story. And maybe, just maybe, he could explain some of the weird hitchhikers on this trip.

"Well," he leaned forward a little, wearily struggled with himself. "I brought Wesakicak into the story to give it some balance. I wanted to explore the mythology of Kiciwaminawak in comparison and contrast with our own stories. I thought it would be interesting to put Wesakicak on Mount Olympus. But he wouldn't stay there. Went off on his own. I guess I should have expected something like that when I started out. Nobody can control Wesakicak."

"So you don't know what Wesakicak is up to?"

"Like I said, I lost control of him."

I was thinking Harold had lost control of more than Wesakicak, when Jules asked, "Tell me, Mr. Writer, you created Charlie and sent him off on an adventure. Why'd you bring him back here?"

"I never brought him here. He just came here."

"Then logically, you would have to agree that if Charlie is in control, you are not. Therefore, this is Charlie's story, not yours."

"This is definitely Charlie's story. But, he's not supposed to end up in a bar in Toronto. Charlie is a bushman, a good hunter, and a provider. He belongs out there where the lakes and rivers meet the forest. He is at one with the trees, with all the animals, with the spirit of the land. He's not meant to be here, not swilling beer in a noisy pub."

"I agree with you. Charlie doesn't belong here." Jules turned slightly so the conversation was between him and Harold. I was left out. "Now the question is, how do we get him to go home?"

"I don't know. I give up. That's what I'm here to talk to him about." Harold turned toward me, let me back into the story. "What'll it take, Charlie?"

Now that I was back in the conversation, I had nothing to say. I sat there without words.

"I'll fix things between you and Thelma." Harold offered.

"Who's Thelma?" Jules wanted to know.

"His sister-in-law. Sometimes she's mean to Charlie."

"Yeah, I guess there is always going to be people like that." Jules lowered his head, looked deep into his beer. The conversation paused. We sat quiet, and the waitress came around again. Nobody wanted anything. She left.

"Okay, Charlie. It's up to you," Harold broke the silence. "What's it going to take?"

"Time," I answered. "Let things unfold as they should, see what happens."

"You don't have time. The publisher is after me to get this finished. We gotta make some decisions here." Harold's agitation was beginning to show.

"It's okay, Harold." Jules was making calming motions with both hands. "Settle down." But Harold wasn't settling down "And you're not helping. You're supposed to help him see the dark side, and here you are buying him alcohol. Listen you two, either you figure out how Charlie goes home in the next couple of pages, or I am going to have to do something drastic."


WESASKICAK WATCHED RAVEN FLAP AWAY THROUGH the trees, rise above them, and spread his wings into a glide. The sun caught him as he banked and reflected the blue shine from his feathers. "Now why was Raven acting that way?" Wesakicak wondered. "We're the same, him and I, brothers. He should have shared his meat with me, like a brother would."

Wesakicak's disappointment didn't last long because the faint smell of oponask fish drew him to a small camp on the high bank of the river. His nose had been correct. Sure enough, there was the fish, split and spread on the end of a Willow pole, held open by smaller pieces of peeled willow woven through the flesh. The white flesh was just beginning to brown over the flame. An occasional drop of oil from the fish dripped into the fire where it sizzled and sent up a little puff of delicious smoke that drifted seemingly straight to Wesakicak.

It was tormenting, but it wouldn't be right to invite himself into the camp. He sat on a rock, very visible, and waited for the invitation. A little black and white puppy came up close, stopped, sniffed, then gave a little bark as if to say, "Do you want to play with me?"

In the camp, a man bent close to the woman sitting by the fire, said a few quiet words, and walked away to stand with his back toward Wesakicak. The fish continued its slow drip, sizzlling above the dancing flames. A butterfly settled on Wesakicak's knee, folded its wings back and rested. "Barely a nibble," Wesakicak thought.

The woman was taking the fish down now, slowly removing the Willow sticks, careful not to rip the tender flesh as she pulled them out. She picked at the occasional piece of fish that was crisped on the Willow and put it lovingly into her mouth. The man came back to stand behind her, watching as she drew the last skewer and set the fish down on the brilliant, green grass between them.

Wesakicak twitched nervously, and brushed the butterfly from his knee in anticipation. It flew up and landed on his finger. The man and the woman were starting to eat. Wesakicak yanked his hand back and left the butterfly with no other choice but to fly away. He coughed, loud and clear, started to stand, then sat back hard on the rock.

"Come, Wesakicak. Come and eat with us." The man was waving at him. "We were teasing you. We knew you were there. Here, sit here and share this fish with us."

"It's not right to tease a hungry man."

"Oh, Wesakicak, you're always hungry. We thought you of all people would appreciate a little humour." The woman placed a generous portion before him.

Wesakicak ate slowly, picked at the fish with his fingers, peeled the tender flesh from the crisped skin, and after he placed each morsel in his mouth, sucked clean each finger, one at a time. The woman smiled at his dedication, caught her husband's eye, and with the smallest of nods drew his attention to Wesakicak, then lowered her head again to her own share of the golden-brown oponask.

They ate in silence until all that was left of the fish was the skin, shimmering in its oil. The man picked it up, plucked off one final piece. "Raven likes this part," he said and carried it to the edge of the clearing where he placed it in the fork of a tree.

"You are good people," Wesakicak said when the man returned.

"You're so polite when you're fed," the woman smiled.

"No, really, it's not common to find such kind people."

"Where have you been travelling, big brother?" Of course the man was speaking Cree and this is only a poor translation. The word he used for big brother was *Nistes* a word of respect. "I am sure that anywhere around here, you would be treated kindly. This is a kind place. Everything is gentle and generous here. Even that fish threw himself on the shore for our breakfast."

"I have never been here before. In all my travels, in all my adventures, I have never seen a place like this since the beginning."

"There is no beginning here." The woman was unbraiding her husband's hair. "This is a place of relatives. Everyone here is a loved one."

"We hear that you've been checking out our grandson, Charlie." The man kept his head steady while his wife worked.

"Yes, yes, Charlie Muskrat." Wesakicak sat up again. He had been lying down after the meal. "He's one of yours."

"He's a good boy. Charlie always tried to be helpful to his Grandparents." The woman was now re-twisting her husband's hair into long neat shimmering black braids.

"How's he doing?" Charlie's Grandfather asked.

"He's doing just fine." Grandma assured him as she gently brushed his cheek with her fingers.

"I'm sure that he is, my wife. I am only asking for news."

"He's fine the last I seen him," Wesakicak told them. "He's looking for something."

"For himself."

"Maybe."

"Sure he is," Grandma finished braiding Grandpa's hair. He gave her a kiss on the cheek in thanks. "It's normal for a young man to go out to find himself."

"He's not that young anymore."

"It's normal for middle-aged men to go find themselves again."

"I suppose, eh?"

"Sure, don't you remember when you were about his age, you took off to La Pas that time."

"Don't remind me." He gave his wife a hug around the waist as she stood beside him, turned and placed his cheek against her stomach. "What about you, Wesakicak. You ever do anything that you wondered about later?" Grandma asked, subtle mischief played around her eyes.

Wesakicak either didn't catch Grandma's hint, or he ignored it, or he caught it and gave a more subtle answer. "I guess I have always been middle aged."

"So, big brother, what is it about our grandson that has you checking him out?" Grandpa asked direct.

"It's that he's half Greek. What are we going to do with him when his wandering around is done?" Wesakicak stretched out again, this time resting on one elbow.

"Well, we've been hoping that he would come here. It would be good to have him around again. He has a long line of ancestors here watching over him. But, of course it's up to him."

"What do you mean, it's up to him?"

"Charlie decides if he wants to live like an Indian or a Greek. It's how he lives his life that makes the difference."

"And if he tries to stay in the middle?"

"I don't think there is a middle place. You are or you aren't."

"What if he decides he wants to come here, and he wants to keep his white ways?"

Grandma sat down beside Grandpa. This idea was troubling. "They wouldn't do that to us again, would they? After all, we let them live with us once, in a place as good as this, and look what they done."

"We're talking about our grandson. He wouldn't do something like that."

"I know. But if Charlie can come here without love of this place, why not others?" She took Grandpa's hand.

He sat silent for a moment, let the thought circulate for a while, let it make another circle, sighed, and placed his cheek on her shoulder.

"So, Don Quixote, what do you want to do now," Jules teased after Harold left.

"Careful now, we don't want that name to stick, or you might become the little guy who rode along with him."

"Might be all right. If I remember, Sancho came out not bad in the end." Jules was leaning back, enjoying himself. "Tell me about the diamonds," he added like an afterthought.

"Well, I wasn't even sure they were diamonds for the longest time. At first I thought they might be just pretty little good luck stones."

"Can I see them?"

I fumbled in the leather pouch, found a few smooth stones between my fingers, and offered my palm to my friend. The stones lay dull, small and simple, in my hand.

Jules leaned forward, plucked one to examine. "So, where did you get them?"

Again the question, the question I did not want to answer, didn't want to answer because the answer was so bizarre, so unbelievable that to tell it would make me look unbelievable.

"Well?" he forced his eyes away from the stone between his fingers and looked directly at me.

I tried to think up a good story, couldn't, and gave in to the questioning eyes.

"They were given to me."

"Some lady gave these to you? What services did you perform?"

"Wasn't a lady."

The eyes were asking "Who then?" And I gave in to them, gave the eyes the story of how I had been sitting alone on a hill, just sitting there in the late summer sunshine, while around me Pines slowly died from dwarf mistletoe. What was I doing there? Just sitting, letting my thoughts play, looking out through the clearing created by a disease that choked trees until they fell in a tumult. Thinking that if this clearing was not so far from home, it would be a good place to get firewood. Thinking that I remembered when this stand of Pine was lush and green, and across the river the Pines were mostly dead. Now across the river, Poplar have taken over and today it is lush and green. Thinking about the flow and flux of things and wondering about the flow and flux of me.

This was the spot where Grandma had brought me to show me where the little people used to dance, where, when she was a little girl, she was not allowed to play.

"But who were they, Grandma? What did they look like?"

"I never saw them. I just heard stories. I did see their tracks one time, though. There in the sand where they had been dancing. Little moccasin tracks about this big." The distance between Grandma's fingers was the length of one of those arthritic fingers.

Her memory faded into the whisper of wind through dry branches as I looked out, down an expanse of wide, winding, brilliant river where Grandpa and I had paddled, past the Willow island and around the bend to where our cabin now stood. My mind wandered through all the years between Grandpa and Grandma and now, across a continent so long ago, and up to the last quiet years of two people keeping each other company as we in our turn became Grandma and Grandpa.

"*So you are not satisfied.*" The voice at my elbow startled me and brought me back to the hill. He walked around and sat cross-legged directly in front of me. The first things I noticed were the moccasins, about the length of an old arthritic finger.

"A leprechaun gave you diamonds." Jules gave me his "can't con me" look.

"Not a leprechaun. A little person. A little Indian person with braids, three of them, two on one side, and one on the other. He talked Cree, old style Cree." I felt I was digging myself deeper. "Leprechauns have green hats and look all funny with big noses and pointy shoes and such. Little people are not like that. Grandma said they'd help you if you ask. We have other stories about them. I know this woman from Green Lake, she told me that, when she was a little kid, at evening these other kids that she didn't know would come out of the forest behind her house and play with her. They would play ball with her. Her parents and her older sister never saw these kids. It wasn't until she was grown up that she realized who those kids were. Said what she remembered the most is that they always brought the ball."

"And one of these little people gave these diamonds to you."

"I didn't know they were diamonds then. I thought they were just stones."

Jules sat silently, waiting for me to go on, polite, patient. I looked around the saloon, at the empty table next to us, at the table beyond, and the woman who laughed too loud with the man who couldn't shoot pool. I felt myself a long way from the hill and that summer afternoon two years past when I sat, head bowed in respect and awe and a little fear, while a little man in a beaded leather shirt smiled up at me. *Charlie, the world is changing. If you don't change with it, you are going to become a memory, just like us. You are going to have to be strong to survive. We'll help you. But it is going to be up to you. Your choice.* He reached down into the Earth to his elbow, felt around and brought up that handful of little stones. *"Here, these will help you. They will make you strong. There is a lesson in here and a test. How you use them will be up to you."*

"Judy made the bag for them."

"Mary made the bag, her name is Mary. I thought by now you would have that right."

"Mary, yeah, Mary made the bag. I never told her what for and she didn't ask. She made me a little leather bag and I put those good-luck stones in there and carried them around."

"Good-luck stones. I'd say these really are good luck." Jules held the white pebble up to the poor light. "Any idea what they're worth?"

"I couldn't even guess."

"Well, Charlie, you got yourself something here. But you know, you can't walk around Toronto with this much money hanging around your neck. Someone is liable to knock you over the head. Maybe I should keep them for you."

"They'll be all right where they are."

"You sure? It wouldn't be a bother to look after them for you."

GRANDMA STIRRED UP THE FIRE, MOVED the coals into a pile and added more wood, hung the blackened can with the wire loop over the flames, and stood there for a few seconds watching the water. "Tea's ready. Want some, Wesakicak?"

"Tea would be just nice after that fish."

"So, you've been checking up on Charlie." Grandpa offered his cup to Grandma in turn, without getting up from where he sat. "How d'you figure he's doing?"

Wesakicak sat back, sipped the tea, and let the flavour flow through him, gentle and sweet. "Oh, Charlie is all right," he answered, all relaxed.

"I agree." Grandma sat, held her tea in both hands. "We've been watching over him too. He'll come through this. Have to have faith."

"It's not what he does on that side. It's what happens to him when he's done that I'm thinking about."

"Well, like we said. It's what he does on that side that will decide what happens after."

I SNEEZED HARD AND SUDDEN, THEN again, shook my head to clear the mist, and looked back at Jules.

"Someone is thinking about you." He offered the old explanation for the sneezes.

I was wondering who would be thinking about me when someone tapped my shoulder. "Mr. Muskrat, my name is Rob Smith from the Department of Indian Affairs."

"I remember you. I'll get those forms in as soon as I get a chance."

"I'm sorry but you must be mistaken. You might have spoken to one of my colleagues. Ron Smith perhaps."

Someone was playing tricks on me. I looked at Rob closer. No, I was certain they were the same, the same shorter-than-short hair, the same blue suit, the same black, plastic-framed glasses, the same hearing device stuck in the same too-large left ear, the same extra-large brief case. But that might be departmental issue. "Okay," I accepted the strange situation. "I'll get those forms filled out for you as soon as I can."

"I am not here about whatever it is you may have arranged with one of my colleagues, Mr Muskrat. The Department has become aware that you have reached middle age and we need to reassess your status."

"My status?"

"Yes, Mr. Muskrat, your birth was registered pursuant to article six point two of the Indian Act. Your death will be arranged pursuant to article ninety-eight of that Act, and now we are required to conduct a reassessment pursuant to article 609 subsection 875 of the Regulations and Policy. Are you still an Indian, Mr. Muskrat?"

My mouth was open but no words were coming.

"You don't have to answer," Jules came to the rescue.

"Failure to co-operate will be noted on the reassessment, but I assure you, Mr. Muskrat, that the Department will conduct this review with or without your co-operation."

Rob moved my beer aside and spread documents on the table as he pulled up a chair. "In fact we are making an exception for you, Mr. Muskrat. These assessments are routinely conducted without the knowledge of the subject. You really do not have anything to be concerned about: Mr. Jules, here, scored quite high on his evaluation a few years ago." Rob removed a pen from his inside breast pocket and clicked it hard. His other hand lay flat and firm on the pile of paper. "Shall we begin?"

There still weren't any words coming from my open mouth.

"I see that you partake in the consumption of alcohol. Very good for you, Mr. Muskrat. That is a point in your favour. How much of your income do you spend on the purchase of alcoholic beverages?"

"I didn't buy this; Jules bought it."

"I am not so concerned about this particular purchase. I am enquiring about your overall practice."

"I can't remember that I have ever bought a drink, not since California anyway."

"Well, to qualify as an Indian you would have to spend an inordinate amount of your income on alcohol. But since you seem to have the ability to manipulate others to make purchases in your favour, I can give you a score of, lets say four point two. Next question. Do you live in poverty?"

"No, I live in Molanosa."

"Charlie has more than enough money." Jules slipped the diamonds he had been hiding in his hand into his shirt pocket.

"Ideally, an Indian should live just below the poverty line. You don't know how much effort the Department makes to ensure that all calculations result in that determination. How far above the poverty line do you live?"

"Oh, he's way above that, almost to the point of rich." Jules grinned.

"That's not good, not good." Rob flipped pages, found a chart and ran his finger down the page. "I'm sorry, but I am going to have to give you a score of minus eight."

The questions followed.

"Are you lazy?

"Are you good for anything?"

"Did you drop out of school?"

"Did you father any children that you are not aware of?"

GRANDMA LOOKED INTO THE RIVER, PEERED beneath the sun sparkle on ripples, and whispered to a Trout. *"Mati Astum."* The Trout swam to the surface, wriggled itself through the shallows until it lay at Grandma's feet. "Thank you," she spoke softly as she gently picked it up.

"Are we going to eat again?" Wesakicak sat a little straighter.

"Someone is coming." Grandpa poured himself more tea from the pail and offered it to Wesakicak.

"Who?" Wesakicak looked around.

"Young William. They went to get him."

Wesakicak looked puzzled.

"Diabetes," Grandpa explained.

Wesakicak still looked puzzled.

"You'll see."

When the Trout was cleaned and spread over the little fire, when the wild turnips and onions and carrots were beginning to boil, and the wooden bowl filled with wild plums and red ripe currants, two men carefully led a third bewildered man into the camp. Grandma and Grandpa greeted him in turn with big smiles and hugs. "Welcome home, William."

"Sometimes it takes a little while until they figure things out," Grandpa told Wesakicak as Grandma helped the man to sit and placed food in front of him. As William ate slowly, glanced around and forced return smiles at the small crowd that had gathered, he began to grow taller, straighter, stronger. The pale-yellow hospital gown became obviously too small and Grandma brought him a buckskin shirt, a pair of soft moccasins and leggings. Soon he was fed, dressed and laughing.

"Wesakicak, was it you that played that trick on us?"

"What trick?"

"Time."

"No, You played that trick on yourself." Grandma offered more berries.

William took a handful. "Too bad, that's probably the best trick there is."

"I don't get it." Wesakicak reached for the bowl.

"They play tricks on themselves while they're on the other side. Some of the tricks are cruel and the cruellest of them all is the trick of time," Grandpa explained.

"I thought it was real, thought it was measured." William sat with his back against a tree, the bowl of berries at his knee. "That was my biggest struggle, not just at the end there in the hospital as my liver and kidneys were shutting down and I wanted more time, more time, more time. My life seemed in those last moments to have been too short. Then there was that time in jail." William tossed a berry in the air and caught it in his mouth. "My little brother thought it would be funny to bring me a book about Time. Hey, what did Einstein do when he got here?" William laughed, tilted his head back and let the laughter rise up from his belly and out his mouth into the air. It echoed in the clearing. Birds chirped their reply. Grandma's smile grew to a grin and a giggle escaped. Soon everyone was laughing with William, who rolled on the ground, kicked his heels into the dirt, tears flooding his eyes.

Wesakicak wiped his eyes, "I don't get it."

"Einstein," someone began but couldn't finish. His laughter cut him off.

Wesakicak spread his hands, palms up, his mouth open and wordless.

"Einstein thought time was real." Words broke through the laugh.

"And numbers." William's laugh let him speak, but only barely before it captured him again and rolled him around. "And logic." William laughed on.

"I still don't get it." Wesakicak didn't know why he was laughing. But it felt good to laugh with people, to share the joy, to be part of the ripple that spread from William slamming his head against the ground, that caused waves that rolled back from the trees at the edge of the clearing added to by the birds and squirrels — waves of laughter that lifted people or laid them onto the grass.

"They all think that time, numbers, and logic are something," Grandma tried to explain. "They spend their lives believing things they made up." Grandma wasn't laughing anymore, but the smile stayed, along with the sparkle in her eye. "They think time has a beginning and an end."

William found his way out of the laugh, but he was still too weak to sit up. He offered from where he lay. "When I was in jail, I wanted time to move fast. When I lay dying, I wanted time to move slow. I kept praying for more time, more time, and time is nothing. I was praying for nothing."

"We heard you," Grandpa continued to smile.

"I should've asked for more life." William sat up. "But what about Einstein, I wonder what he did when he got here?"

"We never saw him. His family must have shared his laugh with him."

"I'd like to see him, talk to him."

"You have lots of time for that." Waves of laughter washed the clearing and echoed across the river.

Rob Smith left at Jules' insistence. It was a little more than mere insistence. I had to assist Rob to the door and hold Jules back. When finally we were seated again and Jules had muttered his last, "Son of a Bitch," we found our way back to our earlier conversation.

"So, what are your plans, Charlie, where do we go from here?"

"Wherever they take us, I guess." I indicated Jules' shirt pocket. He seemed to have forgotten that he had placed the little stones in there.

"Oh, yeah." He felt for the stones and brought them out, placed them in my outstretched hand. "I could look after those for you, Charlie. Toronto has changed since you and I used to hang around here. It's a lot more dangerous. Someone might put a bullet in you for those little beauties."

"Come on, Jules. This is Canada, nobody gets shot here."

"Charlie, what's wrong with your hearing? Don't you hear the gunshots? I thought a hunter like you would know the difference between a shot and a car-door slam."

"I heard them. They come from over to the West, but I figured it was maybe a Metis wedding going on and they were shooting their rifles in the air."

Jules chuckled, "Yeah, if only it was that simple. But serious, Charlie, you need a safe place for them."

I had never considered keeping the little stones safer than they were in the leather bag. Mary sewed that bag. That's right her name was Mary, Mary, Mary. I let her name echo in my mind for a while to keep it there. I know she would have sewn her love into the leather, put her good thoughts there, her warmth. Anything in that bag would feel warm and dry and loved. But maybe Jules was right. A bullet can pierce leather, and love, and even me.

"What do you suggest?"

"I don't know, maybe a safety deposit box or something."

"How do I do that?"

"Just go to a bank, show your ID, fill out some forms and pay the fee."

"ID?"

"Identification. You don't have any ID?"

"I got Robert's driver's licence. It fooled the police the other night."

"Does it have a photo?"

"Yeah, it does, but don't we all look the same to them?"

"Might work."

And it did. My little brother, Robert, now has his very own safety deposit box at the Toronto Dominion Bank on Yonge Street behind the large green TD. It has something valuable in it, but not the little leather bag of stones. Those are still around my neck where they belong. The shiny stainless steel box that slides in and out has all my Canadian Tire money.

When I stepped out of the bank, there was Jules waiting, or maybe standing watch. He showed his relief, "There, Charlie, don't you feel better?" And we walked away together in the afternoon light.

I did feel better. I had done something to make my friend happy. The Metis were celebrating again. Gunshots echoed through the gaps between the concrete, steel and glass. Jules didn't seem to hear them as he strolled the sidewalk, arms swinging. Despite all his motion, he wasn't getting much speed. I slowed my pace so that he could stay with me.

Selling diamonds isn't like selling muskrat pelts. You don't take them to the Hudson Bay Store and watch while the store manager runs his hands over the fur. Usually, the manager is some new guy who doesn't have a clue about size and quality. He'll look in the manual, fumble a tape measure over the pelt, look in the manual, hold the pelt to the light, look in the manual, shake the pelt, look in the manual. I know the manual says he is supposed to listen to the sound the pelt makes when he shakes it with a bit of a snap to determine how dry it is. It's fun to watch him shake the pelt and look in the manual, and the manual doesn't tell him what a good pelt sounds like, it just tells him to shake it and listen.

It's a time of good fun, when a new manager arrives. Makes a guy want to go out trapping, just to bring something in and watch him try to figure it out. You can usually argue that the pelt is worth more than he offers and, of course, he doesn't know, and, if you argue hard, he starts to think maybe he made a mistake, and the price comes up. Everyone seems to get into the action. Some people carry it a little too far and sell the poor guy a road-kill dog and tell him it's a Wolf. A black cat flattened by a car can fetch as good a price as a big Mink. It makes a guy wonder how many of the very fashionable are wearing Fluffy around their necks.

Diamonds are not that much fun to sell. Jules spent all the next day in the yellow pages and on the phone and I watched his television. Television is different than I remembered it. You don't have to wait all week to watch *Star Trek*. Once an hour the Enterprise gets into some mischief, threatened, and nearly spread across the universe in an explosion, or trapped in some kind of space warp. And, a few minutes before the next episode, they escape, only to get into more trouble in the next hour.

I was feeling like the molecules in my brain were floating free of each other after seven episodes. Television overdose left me dazed and feeling a little stupid, like I was high on some cheap drug that sapped my mind, slowed everything down, and sucked out any intelligence that might have been there.

Jules was in a different space, excited and eager and frustrated and angry and disappointed all that the same time. He paced his apartment. Measured the living room in five steps, the kitchen in three, didn't believe the measurement and measured it again, then again. He mumbled. "Mercedes, Royal York, shoes, good shoes. Yeah, good shoes." Finally, he stood and silently stared out the window at the concrete of the next building. I understood this part. When I need to figure something out, I like to look out the window of the cabin across the lake, at the trees on the far shore. Something about looking off into the distance helps to unclutter a mind, especially when you're trying to figure out something in the future. The next building wasn't very far away and I was beginning to wonder how Jules was making out when he turned and stated flatly, matter of factly, "It takes money to make money." He saw something in the short distance. "That's it, Charlie. You need some new clothes. I have to go to work and I can't have you around while I'm working. I won't have time to visit with you anyway, and I know you won't want to sit around in a pool hall and just watch."

Jules came home in the middle of the night. I got up off his couch as he emptied his pockets onto the kitchen table. "Not bad, not bad." He took a wad of twenties from his shirt pocket. He was a different Jules than the one who left the apartment a few hours ago, stronger, straighter, quicker. "A few rough moments. But I got him. The balls bounced for me and not for him. Thing is, Charlie, he was trying to beat the table, trying to win against the balls and the cushion. I was trying to beat him." Jules emptied the other shirt pocket. "And I got him." Jules put both hands on the table and arched his back to stretch out the muscle. "Sometimes the best shot doesn't sink a ball. Sometimes your best shot is one that leaves the other guy in a tough place."

He flipped through the pile of money, sorted twenties and fifties and tens. "Not bad, not so bad at all." He gave me a tight-lipped smile and a little wink. "Better than a grand. Won't take us long like this, Charlie my boy. Won't take long at all."

The next night wasn't so good. "Too cocky, Charlie. I was just too damn cocky. He still had money in his pocket when he left."

The next night was better. "Double or nothing, he said. Double or nothing on one last game. Poor sucker, but it was him that called for it. Wasn't me. I was ready to let him walk, but he called it. I didn't even pretend to be nice. I broke, then shot a perfect game, and he stood there with his hands in his pockets. Should have seen it, Charlie. You should have seen it. Smack, smack, and they went down, one after the other. Then he had to go to an ATM to pay up." Jules drained a bottle of water. "How about you, Charlie? How was your day?" He wiped his mouth with his sleeve.

"A woman saw a ghost."

"What?"

"Yeah, I was out back skinning one of those big fat squirrels when a woman came by and screamed and ran away. She must have seen a ghost because there was nothing else around that could have scared her that much."

"You can't do that stuff, Charlie. You're not at home anymore." A grin gently reshaped Jules' scowling face. "So she screamed a little did she?"

"She screamed a lot."

"So, why were you skinning a squirrel?"

"Well, you're out to all hours trying to make money. I thought I would help. Squirrels are worth a couple bucks, and there's lots of them out there, running all over, big and fat and healthy. So I just put a snare on the handrail. Got a couple of them. Made a real nice lunch."

Jules turned and opened the fridge, glanced in from top to bottom. "Shit, I'll have to get some groceries tomorrow. We're going to have a busy day."

The next day was busy, all right. First we went to the Eaton's Centre for some new clothes. They felt strange on my skin, hard and brittle. Not at all like the clothes that Ester makes for me, or the soft comfortable jeans she finds at the second-hand store. The new shoes pinched as I carefully wrapped my moccasins, folded the flaps and looped the leather strings around the soft bundle of dark brown decorated with dyed porcupine quills before reverently putting them in the shoe box. "Gina made these."

"Mary made them."

"Yeah, Mary made them. Mary, Mary, Mary."

"And they're nice moccasins, Charlie; she did a good job, a real good job. But where we have to go, you have to dress the part. Moccasins and a beaver jacket just won't cut it."

"So, do I look the part now?" I raised my arms and turned around to show my new clothes.

"No, Charlie, store-bought ain't gonna cut it either. For what I have in mind, you need to go to a tailor."

"So what are we doing here?"

"Buying you clothes to go to the tailor in. You can't go to a good tailor shop dressed the way you were. They wouldn't give you the time of day."

All of the walk from the Eaton's Centre to the downtown tailor shop, I apologized. "Sorry, sorry, oops, sorry," as people bumped into me or into the bundles I carried. Most of them were so upset that they walked away without breaking stride, or looking back.

Jules gave the tailor directions, colours, cuts, sounds. "Not too loud. What we're looking for is something conservative. It has to say this is a man who is careful with his money." The little man with the bright-red handkerchief tied around his neck measured and nodded. I worried that a man who dressed the way this one did couldn't possibly make clothes that a person could wear in public.

Jules was more optimistic as we walked down the street toward the tower that looks like a big needle. "Don't worry, Charlie, you'll see. That was the most reputable tailor in town. Now, we still need to get you a watch and a pair of Italian shoes."

"I don't need a watch." I looked over my left shoulder for the sun. It was hiding behind a building. I checked for shadows, but the sun was having trouble shinning through the thick air and the dim shadows were hard to see. "It's about 1:30."

Jules slid up his left sleeve, glanced at his wrist. "You're off, it's only one o'clock."

"Okay, there's a nice Timex." I pointed to the display in the store window.

"Naw, Timex won't do. The people we are going to meet will know a Timex, and a Timex says 'cheap'. You need at least a St. Michel."

In the Swiss Jewellery shop I stopped to look at the display of Swiss Army watches. Jules moved me on toward the back of the store. "Too rugged-looking, you need a watch that says civilized."

The thousand-plus-dollar watch that Jules bought and buckled to my wrist looked very plain and simple. The leather band didn't even have any embroidered stitches, not nearly as fancy as the one Wesley took back from the Black Robes. "I don't get it. How is this going to impress people? Maybe I should keep the receipt so that I can show it off."

"Don't worry about it, they'll know. Two things they'll check out first before they decide to talk to you. What kind of watch you wear and where did you get your shoes. That's not an expensive watch, it's three nights' work. An expensive watch would take me a couple of weeks of hard hustling. But, it'll work to get us in the door." Jules tugged at my sleeve to cover the watch. "Don't show it off, keep it subtle."

"How they going to see it under there?"

"They'll see it."

Mary looked out across the lake, across the melting snow and glare ice into the distance. The sun stood high over her left shoulder, double-bright as it reflected off the ice and snow. She pulled off her hat, a felt and corduroy floppy thing with ear flaps and a wide, cloth, tie-strap, shook loose her hair so that it could feel the wind, and turned her face upward to feel the warmth of the sun.

Charlie was missing this, this time of new life, this time when light returns, when wind does not mean bitter cold. Mary pulled off her mitts and stuck them into the hat, and tucked the hat under her arm as she reached down bare hands into the slushy snow. She stood there in the brightness, in front of the cabin, and rubbed the wet of the melted snow slowly over her face. Just stood there and enjoyed the clean feel of water on skin in wind. Her hands found her throat, lingered there until the ice-water ran down between her breasts, beneath the parka and sweater. She gasped slightly at the feel of chill dripping streaks down her skin.

The zipper of her parka stuck a bit and she tugged harder to undo it, felt a little rise of urgency as she opened the heavy winter coat to expose herself to the warmth of spring. She pulled the parka wider and turned away from the lake toward the sun, toward warmth and light, toward the Grandfather, the Mystery, the brother to her Grandmother, the Moon. She spread herself to this, this beginning of life, this moment a continuation of the first moment. She stood in the now of a spring day and let herself stay there, soaking in it, absorbing it.

*Charlie should be here*, she thought. Then she spoke aloud, "Put those thoughts aside," and again found the quiet now-moment of sun, wind and warmth. She stayed in the moment until it stretched to nothing, until it eased her anxiety and filled her with calm.

Charlie's face appeared, his cheekbones pushing outward from his wide nose, crowding his black, deep eyes. Below the face that caught and stuck in Mary's mind swung the long arms and legs that possessed the sinew strength, the whip strength, but looked like the spindly branches of a Birch. She resisted the image. Turned away to not be caught in it. Missing Charlie would not help him. If she let herself feel her loneliness, it might reach across the distance and draw him home. Charlie needed to go through the passage, follow this path alone, and find his way back, or to wherever he needed to be.

But he or something tugged at her mind and she found herself again in Alcatraz, and Charlie was stepping off the boat. The rock, the prison, had not brought her there. It was not part of being radical, or political, or Native, or even Native American, or Native Canadian. It had nothing to do with the Movement. It was the bridge. The iron bridge suspended by giant spider webs that only looked golden when the setting sun over the Pacific painted it. It was the bridge that brought her to San Francisco. Alcatraz was just another opportunity to see it, to look at it again from another perspective. Mary had been in no hurry. No mad rush to the end. She spent days in the hills looking, absorbing the construction, the height. Other days on the shore, walking under the grid and steel and peeling paint, running her hand over the concrete foundations, until she knew the bridge that spider built, and it was no longer the television image that had set her free. Free to push a few clothes into a tired pack sack and walk out to the gravel road that headed South.

Yesterday the radio said that there were five hundred missing women in Canada. Mary knew where they were. They were there, as invisible as she had been, walking, breathing, feeling ghosts. No one saw an Indian woman for long, or remembered her passing, and Mary walked or drifted to the bridge by the sea, and no one was aware that she had left. That invisibility was the result and the reason. Mary was surprised that there were so many. Maybe that was the only reason someone noticed. Maybe only when there were no Indian women left, someone might notice that they were gone.

Mary remembered her invisibility, the time from before the bridge when invisibility was at its strongest. She stood at the counter and the clerk looked at her, or through her, but did not see her. She waited, patient, checked out the lipstick display. Maybe lipstick would make her visible, give her a mouth, a voice. But what colour goes with brown? Bright red for white women, like a Canadian flag. But brown has no counterpart. And because she was invisible and no one could see her, she put a tube of lipstick in her pocket. And Judge Switzer did not see her, nor did the prosecutor who read the charges on docket day, when the court was full of Indians and no one saw them. "Six months secure," pronounced Switzer. And it was there in Juvy that she saw the television and the bridge.

She had thought she was a ghost, like the ones that followed her and whispered gentle encouragement. She was born that way, invisible and able to see more than anyone else.

When she thought of bringing it to an end, she could not imagine an extension cord around her throat. Not like Aunt Rita in the basement closet for five days and beginning to smell. Not even outside from a tree where the wind might find her. No, Mary wanted to fly up, to soar in the last moment, with her invisible friends around. To go back to them.

Mary could no longer remember the time before this time, but she could remember remembering it, could remember telling her mother about how she came here. "It was all white there. I was up somewhere high and looked down through a crack. I knelt and looked down and I could see little houses and cars and little trees. I wasn't trying to come here. I just fell. It was like someone sucked me through a straw and I was on this side and it was all black here." Her mother continued to braid her hair but now the fingers worked smoothly, gently, stroking rather than pulling. The memory of that earlier time, and the time before that she knelt and looked through the crack were not available. Mary could not draw them back up. All she had was the memory of the telling, and the memory that she had not made it up.

Raven cawed, loud, directly over her head. Mary looked up as Raven winged away toward the lake. She lowered her eyes toward the lake again to see a Bald Eagle strut across the ice toward the fish left there for her. "You've been so long coming back that Raven thinks those fish are his." Mary smiled at the sight of her Grandmother Bald Eagle. She had been away for too long.

"Do you want to lift that net?" Thelma came and stood beside her older sister and shared the view of Bald Eagle and Raven dancing around the fish left on the ice.

"In a while. Let's leave them for a bit."

"Nice, eh?"

"It is."

Both women stood in silence, enjoyed the warm South Wind on their hands and faces and in their hair.

"Charlie should be here."

"Yeah, he could lift the net, clean the fish, feed the dogs, go out and catch us a few muskrats. I'm hungry for a smoked muskrat. But, you said you can't let yourself miss him too much."

"I know, its just spring, and Charlie really enjoys this part. But, you're right. I can't let myself miss him or he'll hear me and come home."

"Do you think he can still hear you, that he isn't so caught up in his little adventure that he's deaf to you?"

"He can hear me." Mary's voice was certain, calm, quiet.

She spoke so softly that a moment of silence followed; even South Wind held her breath while the women stood shoulder to shoulder, until Thelma asked, "What do you think he's up to?"

A mischievous smile followed a long "Oooh. He's up to no good, getting himself into and out of all kinds of trouble."

"Good old Charlie, but aren't you worried he'll find another woman. I mean it could happen. He's not that ugly and he has lots of money, you said."

"That's not what I worry about as much as who is going to come back, who is Charlie going to be when he comes back?"

"*If* he comes back."

"Yeah, if he comes back. There's a chance of that too."

"Wouldn't be so bad." Thelma put her hands on her wide hips.

Just then Eagle jumped over Raven, and grabbed at the fish. The women laughed together; South Wind stirred, light and quick. The sun reflected sparkles of tiny brilliance on the melting snow. Raven and Bald Eagle danced around the fish, stepped in for a fast snap, and back, and around.

Mary let the laugh trickle out and was still smiling when she heard Thelma whisper, "Instead of calling Charlie home, why don't you call Julian?"

I don't know why the thought of Julian came into my head, but I found myself looking around for him wondering if my son would recognize me in the new clothes.

Jules stopped a few steps ahead of me and turned back.

"What?"

"Nothing." The streets were full of strangers. Julian was not among them.

"Well, come on, then."

We did, we went on. My new Italian shoes, almost as comfortable as moccasins, met the wet concrete, the handmade suit hung gently from my shoulders, wrapped itself around me. It felt as comfortable as a shirt from a second hand store, all broken in and gentle.

As Jules and I walked together, avoided other pedestrians, stopped and waited for electronic permission to cross a street, for the green man to flash, I wondered where Julian might be. Was he all right? Of course he was. If Julian was in trouble, I would know. I would just know. It didn't feel like something bad. I let my thoughts cast around for him as cars whizzed by, past the tips of my soft leather shoes at the edge of the curb. He refused to appear and I let him go with a wish for his well-being.

I could hear the gunshots again and I wondered how long the Metis celebrated a wedding in Toronto. Would they wear their buckskins here in the city, or would they wear Italian shoes instead of moccasins?

"Do you have the key?"

I gave Jules a blank look.

"The key to the safety deposit box."

I looked over his head at the large green TD before I remembered what he was talking about. "Yeah, right here." I patted the little leather bag.

"Well, maybe you should go in and get about half a dozen or so. All we want is a sample. Just pick out a few, not the biggest ones, but not all small either."

The people at the bank were much friendlier today, though all their courtesy took longer. I had to wait while the clerk who showed me into the safe the other day ran to find a manager. I've never seen a man behave like that before. The manager acted like he was a long lost relative and I was the family patron. "Right this way, Mr. Muskrat."

I felt embarrassed for him and really hoped that he would not kiss my Italian shoes that he kept looking at.

He rushed an older lady out of the safe. I gave her a smile as she tried to stuff her purse while the manager, holding her elbow, nearly dragged her out the narrow steel doorway.

"Take as much time as you need, Mr. Muskrat." He turned his back and stood solid guard at the door. It did not take me long to look at the Canadian Tire money, count the forty-seven cents and put it back in the box. The manager was very polite as he walked me to the door and then I was back on the street where Jules waited.

"How'd it go?"

"Strange."

"Get used to it."

Wesakicak waited for Grandpa to finish the paddle. He did not have the patience for this sort of work — find a tree that held a paddle inside itself, ask the tree for the paddle, wait for the answer, cut the tree, find the paddle in the wood again, and whittle away the parts that were not paddle. Grandpa sat in the middle of a pile of shavings and stroked a blade down the knot-free wood — smooth strokes, gentle strokes filled with kindness and thanks, thanks to the tree for the wood, thanks to the wood.

The canoe had taken long enough to build: ask each Birch tree for some of its bark; ask Spruce for some of its gum, a few of its roots to sew it all together; ask Willow for some of its branches; bend and shape and stitch; speak quiet, gentle words to the bark, the roots, the branches bent to make canoe ribs. There it lay on the shore of the river, its pure white skin of squares marked out by amber spruce gum reflecting the brilliance of the sun and water.

Wesakicak paced, came up again from the river and the canoe, and stood again behind Grandpa, looking over his shoulder. "Is it ready?"

"Not yet."

"How long?"

"Soon." Grandpa slid the blade against the wood, pulled it in a long easy glide along the shaft of the to be paddle. A strip of wood, curved and coiled, rolled up and fell away. Grandpa turned the paddle-to-be a fraction and drew the blade again.

"*Astum*, Wesakicak." Grandma called Wesakicak toward the Wigwam. "Come help me fix this door. It has come loose again."

"You guys work all the time." Wesakicak held the door in place while Grandma adjusted the woven willow-bark ropes so that it hung straight.

"Not all the time. We play and eat and tell stories too."

"I thought you wouldn't have to work here."

"Why not. Work is good."

"But, when you were on the other side, you had to work all the time."

"We didn't have to. We thought we did, and sometimes we thought work was something bad, forgot that it was a gift."

"What's the sense of coming here, then. You still have to work."

"Don't have to. That's the difference. Here we can work if we want to. There, other people made us work, or we made ourselves work and forgot that work was a gift. See this rope?" Grandma snugged the woven Willow bark against the pole that held up the door flap. "It was fun to make this. All the joy I felt while my fingers braided this rope together is still here. You can feel it. Here, touch it."

Wesakicak took the end of the rope in his hand. A sensation tingled, as though the rope were alive, like holding a baby bird that slept peaceful in his palm. "So that's the difference, then? On the other side your work is for nothing. Here things have spirit."

"Things have spirit on that side too. It's just that people have gotten away from knowing it. When I used to sew, especially moccasins, I put good things into my sewing, good thoughts so that Charlie or Grandpa wouldn't trip. That doesn't happen anymore. A lady came over not so long ago and she had on a pair of shoes that she couldn't walk in. Most people don't have anything on their feet. I guess if it doesn't show in the casket it doesn't matter. This one guy came wearing a suit, a nice suit, double breasted, good cloth. But it was way too big for him and it had been cut up the back and tucked around him. He looked real nice from the front, from the waist up. But he had to walk around barefoot with his backside sticking out until his relatives found him."

"His family on that side didn't care about him."

"No, I think they did their best. They just didn't know any better. To them it was important that he look his best on his final day laid out in the chapel. They got him ready for that final day and didn't know enough to get him ready for his journey."

"Hey, Wesakicak, *Cheestee*," Grandpa held up the finished paddle. Its yellow-white wood flashed in the sunlight.

"It's light." Wesakicak hoisted it, flipped it up and down. Tried a practice stroke, pulled the paddle through the air, and then held it loosely in both upright palms to check its perfect balance. "This will make paddling easy."

"Not that we have muscles to get sore, anyway." Grandpa brushed shavings from his leggings. "Should we try it out?"

Wesakicak carried the bow while Grandpa held the stern of the canoe clear of the ground until they reached the river and waded out into calf-deep water before gently setting the canoe down. It floated, light as a leaf. Wesakicak sat in the bow while Grandpa paddled, listening to the sound of each stroke *swish*, *swish*. The canoe turned gracefully toward the left, then Grandpa steered it in a long arch back toward the shore where Grandma stood smiling, approving. He quickened the pace of the swish and the canoe sped straight, flat on the water. He stopped paddling as they neared the shore, but the canoe did not slow. Wesakicak was forced to jump out and grab the bow thwart to keep it from running into the ground.

"Like a dream," Grandpa said as he and Wesakicak carried the canoe back up the riverbank to set it again on the grass. "Paddles like a dream."

Grandma turned away, her smile fading as she walked toward the river. Her smile that had been generated by Grandpa's and Wesakicak's accomplishment became a show of concern. She walked out into the water, bent and gently picked up a bubble, a tiny blue bubble. She carried it between her thumb and finger and held it up to the light. Its colour flowed in easy swirls, reflected the sun and the trees and the river and, deeper below the surface, something more.

"What is it?" Wesakicak asked Grandpa.

"Charlie's memory." They watched Grandma carefully place the bubble into a small beaded leather bag hanging in a tree. "It will be here when he gets here."

"I don't understand."

"Charlie has holes in his memory. The bubbles of his memory come here and we keep them for him," Grandma explained.

"Was it a good memory?" Grandpa asked.

"Not really."

"Well, maybe it's a good thing that he doesn't have to carry it around with him."

THE PEOPLE AT THE CAR RENTAL place were quick. Everything they did, they did at double pace. They even spoke fast. "Yes, Mr. Muskrat. Your assistant reserved a car for you. If you will sign here, I will have the car brought around to the front." I scrawled my name on a piece of paper; a young lady came in and handed me a set of keys. Each key had a symbol on it, kind of like the peace signs we used to wear, but with a line missing. I handed her the pen.

"Thank you for choosing Mercedes, Mr. Muskrat. We hope you have a pleasant stay in Toronto."

Jules drove slow, made that car with the slippery leather seats do graceful things in downtown traffic. I insisted that we drive by Thunder to pick up the Johnny Cash CDs. Jules checked his watch. "Well, okay, but we have to be at the hotel in a little while."

Thunder didn't seem to mind that I was riding in a fancy car. He stood at the curb with his front wheels turned toward the street, ready to go. I was a little worried that he might be jealous, but he just stood there, let me fumble for the music, push the rifle further under the seat where it would be completely out of sight of anyone who happened to look through the window. "I won't be long, Buddy." I whispered as I made sure the door was shut securely.

The Royal York is not worth the money Jules paid for the suite of tiny rooms. The old stone hotel might be famous, have a history, a distinct presence in the city, the staff might be proficient, polite, unobtrusive, but the rooms are far too small for the hotel to charge the amount they ask at the heavy, wood counter downstairs.

I had barely examined the rooms, not that there was much to examine, when the phone rang. Jules answered it.

"Come right up, Mr. Hesse." He hung up the phone and asked, "Ready?"

"I guess." Not sure what I was ready for.

Mr. Hesse did not see my watch or my new shoes. He didn't look. When we shook hands, he looked into my eyes. I could feel him in there like a question. He squeezed my hand. I responded with care. His hand, after all, was without calluses. He had never held an axe handle, or a skinning knife.

"Herman," he offered to my, "Nice to meet you, Mr. Hesse."

His assistant was as tall as Thelma but much thinner. Her tight, leather jacket showed her shape like a second skin. "Celina," she said as we shook hands. Now here was someone who might have used an axe, or a skinning knife, or a fleshing bone, but somehow I doubted it. More likely a sword or a club. This was not a woman that I was anxious to get to know. She stood easily, close to the door, and smiled whenever I looked her way, a smile that was merely acknowledgement of my gaze, nothing more. At one point during that afternoon exchange in the little hotel room, I felt her behind me and turned in time to catch her eyes on my back. Wolverine eyes. No, I think I would rather take on a pair of Wolverines before I tried anything funny with Celina.

The folding glass table with stainless steel light attachments that Herman set up, came in a case that seemed too small to hold it. It held my attention more than the six thumbnail size stones that rested on it. I was thinking it would be handy for skinning squirrels or weasels. We would have to get electricity into the cabin for the lights, but maybe Grace would like a generator out back. It would have to be quiet. That was her complaint about places that used generators: "How can Uncle Ben hear himself think with that racket?"

Yeah, a nice quiet generator, a skinning knife that stayed sharp, a glass table with bright lights, and I could skin muskrats after five-thirty when the sun went down on winter evenings. No more coal oil lamps and squinting.

"You enjoy doing that don't you." Thelma poured her sister a fresh cup of tea. Mary looked up from the half-skinned muskrat, puzzled.

"You like being all bloody and smelling like a bush woman."

"Hey, rich white women pay a lot of money to smell like musk."

"But they don't have blood and fat under their fingernails."

"They can't have everything. How's the fire under the smoke rack?"

"Just put some more on. Green poplar, like you ordered."

"Don't pretend like you don't enjoy this too. I saw you taking a muskrat out of a trap today. You weren't all fussy, scared to touch it. You were having as much fun as I was." Mary made a few final delicate cuts around the nose of the muskrat, separated the pelt from the body, shook it out and ran her fingers over the thick, shiny fur. "Nice one. Here you go, put this on the smoke rack and we'll have it tomorrow for breakfast. I'll finish stretching this pelt." She handed the muskrat body to her sister.

"How much do you think we'll get for those six pelts?" Thelma took the muskrat.

"Oh, depends. Maybe twenty bucks at best. Not like it used to be. Used to get up to five, six dollars for a nice muskrat."

"Twenty dollars, for two people working all day. That's only a little better than a dollar an hour."

"You didn't count the fun we had. How much was all the laughing worth?"

"Like when you fell through the ice?" Thelma laughed again. "I can still see you with one leg down the hole, the other stretched out on the ice."

"Not so bad, it was only one leg." Mary shivered at the memory of the cold water on her thigh. "Charlie has fallen all the way through. Came home as wet as the muskrats in his pack sack." She pulled the pelt tight over the stretcher board, shaped it to fit, and tapped a nail through the hide into the board to hold it in place.

"Was he laughing?"

"Of course."

"Charlie's so stupid he'd laugh at the end of the world."

"Be nice." Mary's voice was stern. "Charlie's not stupid. His brain doesn't work all the time, but he's not dumb. He laughs at things because that's the way he is. That's the real Charlie showing through."

"I know. I like Charlie. It's just that he's so irresponsible. You'd think at some point he'd grow up."

"Charlie's as responsible as he can be. Imagine what it must be like for him. Imagine having holes in your memory and your brain tries to fill in the empty spaces by making stuff up. Charlie doesn't lie. He tries to tell the truth. He's trying hard. It's just that he doesn't have everything that we have."

"FAS sucks."

'That's too easy. That's putting the blame somewhere. We can't fix Charlie, that's just the way he is."

"I'm not blaming, not even his mom. It's just that it must be hard for you, living like this, never knowing."

"I'm okay. I really like the way we live." Mary finished wiping the grease from the pelt and leaned the stretcher against the wall where it would dry. "Imagine if it was you or me. What would it be like if your brain betrayed you. It says something for Charlie that he laughs at it instead of getting angry."


"COME ON, WESAKICAK, LET'S GO." WILLIAM stood by the canoe with a small bundle under his arm.

"What's your rush? You just got here." Wesakicak stayed sitting just back of the cook fire, that magical flicker that turned a fish into a golden-brown delicacy. Nothing was on the fire at the minute, but the potential remained.

"I want to go back." William remained standing, hoping that his stature would urge Wesakicak to move.

"This is a nice place, good food, good weather. Why don't we stay for a while?"

"I want to go back. I still have things to do." William took a step towards the canoe. "I'm not satisfied yet."

Grandma stood, slowly walked over to William and wrapped her arms around him, kissed his cheek. "You be careful over there, and we'll be here when you get back."

"You and Grandpa are staying?"

"We're done, we have enough to keep us for a long time here. Oh, at some point we might go back, but for now we're done. Just going to hang out here, relax, eat good for a while."

"Me too." Wesakicak sat firmer on the ground.

"You won't last." Grandma came and stood behind Wesakicak. "You have too much adventure in you. Remember when the world was new and you and your brother Mahikan walked all over it. Remember when you took on the water cats and when you tricked the ducks and geese. That was a classic. You can't do that here. You can't be the trickster here. There's nothing to trick. If you want to eat duck soup, just ask a duck to swim in the pot and he will."

"Oh, all right, then." Wesakicak began to rise. Grandma put her hands under his arms and helped him to his feet.

"When you see Charlie again, give him our blessing." Grandma patted Wesakicak on the back.

The canoe trip across the river was uneventful, a pleasant paddle. Wesakicak looked down into the water, searched the riverbed for his mother's head, but it wasn't there. Must have been a different river where Pelican dropped her. He looked back toward Grandma and Grandpa standing hand in hand on the shore. Grandpa waved, a long easy motion over his head: farewell, good luck, good journey. William sat eagerly in the bow of the canoe, eyes on the far shore. The distance between the Ancestors and Future generations is not far, a short paddle in a light, fast canoe.

When the canoe touched the far shore, William jumped out and ran towards a group of young people. He became younger as he ran until when he reached them he was sprinting like a teenager.

"Am I too late?"

"No, there's still time." A young woman moved aside and let William into the circle. "Are you going?"

"I sure hope so." William knelt at the edge of the little hole, not much bigger than a Rabbit might make, and looked down.

"I'd be happy to go, if you don't want to," a young man offered.

"Me too"

"Or me."

"We all want to be Charlie Muskrat's grandson," the young woman sighed.

"Charlie Muskrat's grandson. This is going to be good." William leaned forward, eased his head and shoulders into the hole and, like a muskrat entering water, he dived into the Earth.


I WATCHED HERMAN MOVE THE STONES around on the fancy glass table. It was as though he was playing some sort of game against himself. The little room high in the Royal York Hotel held its breath through those long moments. Not that the room ever had life to it, not like a cabin that breathes and welcomes a tired man home, and feels like the warmth of a woman. I looked around while Herman examined stones and squiggled numbers on a small square pad, as he kept score in the glass bead game.

Jules, for all his confidence, looked out of place as he stood with his hands behind his back, a soldier standing easy.

Celina stood likewise, but kept her hands in view. She looked like she was part of this room: unwelcoming, cold, and indifferent. Herman hunched over the table, the bright lights caught his brushcut hair, turned it a sharper blond. The game he played did not last long and I am not sure who won. I think I might have. In the end there was a pile of one-hundred dollar bills on the glass table that was now mine. Herman and Celina left with six stones in a small felt-lined case and Jules relaxed back into being a normal friend and advisor.

"Don't spend it all in one place." I felt his hand on my shoulder. I wasn't looking at the money. I was amazed at the table and how easily Herman agreed to part with it. "Throw in the table and you have a deal," I'd countered his offer of a hundred and ninety-two thousand.

"Deal." And it was done, and Herman and Celina were gone, and there was only Jules and me, and the table, and the money to count. "One for you, one for me, one for you, one for me."

"No, Charlie. I don't need half. Just my investment back and maybe a little bit of profit. But not half."

"Naw, I don't think so. Half seems better. One for you, one for me." And that is the way it went until there were two piles and I asked, "What are you going to do with your share?" I was really asking for some idea about what I was going to do with my share.

"I think I'll begin with a celebratory bottle. This calls for a twelve-year-old scotch."

"Make that two bottles." I added, as Jules called room service.

I DIDN'T FEEL SO GOOD WHEN I woke up. Pale light oozed through the window and filled the room, pressurized it, replaced the air with its dullness. My skull was lined with fuzz, or rabbit fur, or something that slowed my thoughts. My stomach was lined with a different kind of fur, maybe weasel or wolverine, something slick and shiny and bitter.

Jules lay sprawled on the bed in his room. I glanced through the partly-open door. A woman as tall as Celina curled in a long coil on the other half of the bed. I pulled the door closed quietly. None of my business.

"Hey, Charlie." A woman's arm waved over the back of the sofa. "How's the funny man this morning?" She sat up, threw her legs over, and stood, stretched, arms above her head, reaching naked to the ceiling. The stretch raised her breasts, lengthened her legs and showed her rib cage and tan lines.

"I have to pee." She gathered together an arm load of clothes from the back of the sofa and sprinted to the bathroom.

I needed air.

Toronto streets are busy early. Fast-walking people, eyes straight ahead, sidestep each other. A woman pounded the concrete in a stationary jog at the curb, waiting for the green man to flash before she bounced up and down across the street, not travelling any faster than the walking pedestrians. I suppose city people need exercise too.

"Got a dollar or two for a fellow down on his luck?" The man looked to be about my age, though his life must have been much more difficult than I experienced. The lines in his face were deeper than mine. His eyes were harder. I looked to the outstretched hand. It was a hand that had worked at some time, work that took the first finger at the knuckle and mangled the others.

"Sure." I found a bill in my shirt pocket and put it in the hand.

"Hey," he yelled. "What the fuck you trying to do? Give a guy a heart attack?" He held the brown hundred-dollar bill in both hands, stretched it, held it up to the light, to where the hard eyes could find it, made sure it was real. "You can't do shit like this to an old guy like me."

"You're not so old."

"You don't know, Buddy. You just don't know."

"Okay." I didn't know what else to say.

"Well I guess I am going to eat good today. Thank you very much, sir." He stretched his hand out again. This time to shake mine, to pump my hand up and down, firm, fair, dignified. "Thank you, sir. Bless you and your family."

The street became more comfortable then, friendlier. The rabbit in my brain settled down. The weasel in my stomach curled up and went to sleep. I walked easily on the concrete, Italian shoes as light as moccasins. It *is* easy to make hard faces smile, jump and spark. Hand, after hand, after hand, pumped mine. The sun found its way from behind a cloud and bathed the streets with light and warmth.

I was wondering how this story was going to turn out. Something magical was happening. A mystery was beginning to reveal itself, but the rabbit was still there, in the way. I could not see how I would be, how I would live in this new world.

I stood there on Yonge Street, that section close to downtown where the little shops stand shoulder to shoulder, where the people walk slowly and look in windows. What are they looking for? Maybe the same as me, looking for answers. A bell jingled as a man in a light-grey overcoat came out of a bookstore, tucked his package into a large pocket. He nodded as he came past me.

A bookstore. Maybe there were answers in there.

"Can I help you with something?" the thin man with the blond ponytail suddenly appeared in front of me.

"Uh, yeah, looking for a book." Of course I was, I was in a bookstore, what else would I be looking for?

"Any book in particular?" he was patient despite my dumb answer.

I was thinking maybe psychology or maybe self help; *Life for Dummies* or something.

I didn't have time to answer before he reached over to a shelf and pulled out a little black and red book. "Might I recommend Harold Johnson's *Charlie Muskrat?*"

I flipped through the book, my heart pounding, read the section about picking up Wesakicak hitchhiking, flipped forward, read the part about Winnipeg, about Mary. Yeah, Mary, Mary, Mary. Maybe I could use this book to fill in the empty spots. It could be my memory. A little clumsy, but it might work. If only it had the part about when Mary, Mary, Mary and I first made love. I skimmed through it. It didn't go back that far. Then a thought, a frightening thought slipped out from behind the sleeping rabbit. "How does this end?"

I flipped to the back of the book. Eyes closed, silent prayer, "Let it be good." Eyes open, the page lay white in front of me. I started to read:

*Charlie let his last breath go. Let his heart give one final strong drumbeat in the song of his life. He saw the light and walked steadily toward it. Two helpers came and held him by each shoulder, helped him as he floated up above the Earth, through a wall of fire and across the long gap to where Grandpa and Grandma waited for him.*

The book hit the floor with a bang that brought me back to the bookstore. The man with the ponytail looked disappointed. "Don't you like it?"

"No, it's fine. I have to go."

Then I was on the street again. The sun was gone, behind a cloud or something, something dark. The Metis celebration continued with the occasional crack of a gunshot. The thought of their party did not lift my dread. I was going to die. Would I make it home to . . . Oh, what is her name? I felt my shoulders sag, dragged down by the weight around my heart, around my lungs. I forced air into my body. Drew deep against the resistance, released it with a sigh, forced my lungs to accept another deep breath. I breathed. I was alive. The street returned to my vision: cars, people, buildings, signs, posts, and a ragged man with his hand out.

"Oh, Mary, you're a grandma." Thelma gently pulled down the soft, fluffy, blue blanket to expose the face of the sleeping baby. Mary moved in on her sister, moved her aside, not with any rudeness, without an elbow; with her presence, with her new power, the power of a Grandmother.

"Thank you, Julian." The words barely escaped from the intense rise of emotions that lifted Mary, filled her, and made her head and heart light. The baby woke at the attention, woke with a tiny yawn first before he opened his eyes. "He looks like Charlie," Thelma offered over Mary's shoulder, her cheek close to her sister's ear.

"He looks like someone. But it isn't Charlie." Mary searched her memory for the face. It was an old face she looked for.

"I think he looks like his dad." Brenda offered. The baby bounced slightly as she repositioned her tired arms.

"Let me." Mary reached for the bundle.

"Where's Dad?" Julian asked from his place slightly outside the circle of women.

"He'll be home in a couple days." Mary did not look up from the baby in her arms.

"You sure?" Thelma looked puzzled toward her sister.

"Yeah, he's almost done. A couple days."

"Good. I took a couple weeks off work. We were hoping to stay out here, if that's okay. We wanted some quiet time."

"Of course." Mary still did not look at her son who now stood with one arm around Brenda's waist, together, a couple, parents. "No one has been in your cabin since you left. You might have to sweep up after the mice, but everything is there."

The hand held out to me was old, a hand that worked with basic tools, axe, shovel, hammer, a hand that stroked a woman's hair in kindness, a hand that knew the feel of paddle blisters, the feel of firewood splinters at forty below, a hand that pulled snow-shoe laces tight, and wrapped around a hot cup of tea poured from a can on a winter camp fire. I looked from the hand to the face. It was familiar, but I couldn't place it. The lines and folds told a long story, a story of a journey from somewhere to here. Somewhere else this face was a grandfather, a wise uncle. I wondered if the old man knew the end of his story as I continued to replay the end of mine.

"*Tansi Moshum.*" I offered.

He answered in English. "Not good, Grandson." He looked at the hundred-dollar bill I crumpled into his hand. "But things are looking better."

"It won't bring you a longer life or happiness."

"I've had a long life, all I want now is a hot meal."

I caught a shadow behind the old man, a familiar shy shape, one that normally disappears quietly into the trees. Mahikan what are you doing here in the city? Wolves belong in the forest. And why with this old man?

I stepped back a bare half step and looked again at the old man. My memory trickled a story. Wesakicak and his little brother Mahikan, and Mahikan howled all night in loneliness for his brother, cried so long and so loud that he turned into a Wolf.

"Your hands almost fooled me, Wesakicak." Courage to face the Trickster, or foolishness? "They look like a worker's hands, not the lazy Trickster always taking the easy way."

"No tricks, Charlie; these are my hands." He held them out. "See the dirt under the nails, that is from Muskrat and the making of Turtle Island. See the scars from fighting the Water Cats."

"Where are the feathers from when you wrung the necks of the ducks and geese?"

"You people only remember the funny stories, the foolish ones. Why don't people remember the hero stories. How many times did I save the two-legged? Who brought you dogs to help you? Who made this island for you to live on?" Wesakicak pouted, injured.

"I'm sorry, Grandfather. As you probably know, my memory is not that good."

Wesakicak's face brightened. The shadow of Mahikan lay down, rested on concrete. "I have something for you, Grandson." Wesakicak fumbled in the deep pocket of the overcoat that hung from him like an old blanket thrown over a Willow bunch, reached way down into the coat until his elbow disappeared. "Something I found in a tree." He drew out a leather bag. I recognized Grandma's beadwork, flowers of red and yellow, woven together with green and white. "Do you have something to trade for this?" He held the bag up straight in front of me.

"What's in it?"

"Oh, Charlie, this is good." His voice held a hint of the trickster "You're gonna like this." He drew the bag back, pulled on the leather thong with both his teeth to open it. Then he was holding a little blue bubble up in front of my nose. I leaned back a little to focus. Something below the surface of the bubble swirled.

"What's this?

"Your memory."

"My memory?"

"Yeah, your memory. This one is last night." He drew it back and looked into it. "Good times in here." He sounded like a salesman. "Do you want to see?"

"Not really."

"Well, how about this one?" He dug deeper into the bag for another bubble. "How about when you first kissed Mary?" He held the bubble up in front of my nose and pinched it until it popped. The memory of that morning hit me with a slam, but Wesakicak had it backwards. It was not the first time I kissed Mary, it was the first time Mary kissed me. I could feel her soft moist lips on mine. I could feel the sunshine, and the salty breeze from the Pacific pushing my hair into my face and the smell of Mary's hair, and joy and excitement, and Mary's hand pressing softly on my chest, and I wanted to stay there but Wesakicak was offering me another bubble.

"What do you have to trade for the memory of the first time you and Mary made love?" The salesman was having fun with me.

"Anything . . . Everything." And he could have his way with me. But what to trade? I didn't have anything near the value of the bubbles. "All I have are a few little stones." I offered pitifully.

"Well, okay. For you, Charlie. But don't be telling people that I made such a poor deal. I have to be careful of my reputation you know."

"It's all I have." I drew my bag from under my shirt, raised my chin to lift it out past the lump in my throat.

"One for one. Your little, ugly stones for beautiful bubbles filled with wondrous things." Wesakicak did not have to continue the act of the salesman. I was sold.

I traded thirty-three stones for thirty-three blue bubbles. There were seven bubbles left in Wesakicak's bag at the end of the exchange. They were memories I did not want: last night, someone named Bert Russel that Wesakicak thought might be important but I declined, the time I chopped my foot. I didn't need that memory. I had the scar.

The lamp hiss ebbed to silence as night flowed into the cabin until Julian stood alone in the dark. He carefully found his way, feet moving slowly over the bare, wood floor away from the gas lamp hung from a centre pole, toward the bed where Brenda waited naked under layers of quilts and blankets. He wrapped his arms around her, pulled himself closer until their bodies touched from toe to shoulder, until their bodies fit the curves and angles of each other. He gripped a quilt and tucked it tight behind her to keep out the chill. She did the same for him and they waited motionless for a while, for their body heat to warm the cold bed, until their private cocoon of cotton and wool became comfortable.

"You're a good man, Julian." The warmth of Brenda's breath touched Julian's throat, her cheek in the hollow of his shoulder. "I'm glad you built your own cabin."

"It was Mom's idea. I was about fourteen when all of a sudden she got it into her head that young boys becoming men need their privacy. Dad never said much. He just took me out and we started cutting trees and peeling logs. Next thing I knew, I had a cabin."

"So where is your dad?"

"Don't know. Mom said he went hunting, but it sounds like he's been gone for a while. It's hard to get a straight answer out of her and Aunt Thelma."

"I noticed that. It's like they talk to each other without words."

"They've always done that. Aunt Thelma comes to visit during school breaks, Mom gets all happy, and they don't say anything to each other, just hang out. Then Thelma goes back South. I used to wonder if she talked to her students, or if they all sat quietly in a classroom and did their own thing."

The cocoon was warm. Brenda moved slightly away from Julian so that she wasn't talking to his chin. "What about your dad?"

"Oh, nothing strange about Dad. He always finds an excuse to be away from home when Thelma is here. Gives them space I guess."

"But, what's he like?"

"Dad." Julian found some space in the blankets that had warmed. He relaxed into it, turned onto his back and looked to the ceiling, at the pole rafters he and his father had put in place.

He could see them now that his eyes had adjusted to the dark. "Dad's a little different. I used to wonder why other kids' dads had jobs and mine didn't, why my dad trapped and fished instead of going off to work. But I tell you, now that I'm working, I really envy him. He has a good life out here."

"But it's not for you."

"It could be." They laid in silence for a moment, each with their own thoughts, each with their own view of the ceiling. "But we have Namia now, you have your job, I have mine. Maybe we could retire out here some day."

"You could bring your computer out here. Connect by satellite. You're always talking about how now it's possible to work anywhere in the world."

"Naw, it would change it too much."

Brenda's voice held a hint of a tease. "You just don't want to give up your Starbucks coffee, that's all."

"And the central heat," he moved closer to Brenda's warmth, "and running water, and the theatre, and you wouldn't be able to go shopping whenever you wanted."

"Yeah, I don't think I could chop wood the way Thelma does anyway." She turned into his shoulder again, snuggled down into the covers. "See you in the morning, my love. I'm glad your mom is keeping baby with her tonight. I need the rest."

I wanted to pop all of the bubbles at once. Just grind them all together and stick my nose into the bag of bubbles. But not here, not on the street. Most of these memories had forests in them, and rivers and lakes and ocean. Maybe I would remember the mountains. I turned back the way I had come, toward the tall building that looked like a needle. The hotel and the keys to Thunder would be a little to the West of it.

"I like Brenda." Thelma closed the door to the fireplace, firelight through the glass window danced on her legs and feet. Mary didn't stir.

"You going to hold that baby all night?"

"Maybe." Mary looked up from the bundle. "You're just jealous because you don't have a grandchild." Mirth splashed her words.

"Well, if I did have a grandson, I wouldn't let them name him Namia, especially if his last name is going to be Muskrat. Imagine when he goes to school with a name like that, Namia Muskrat. I can just hear the other kids calling, "Am I a muskrat?""

"That's easy to fix. We just give him a new name."

"Too late. They already registered him."

"Doesn't matter what the government thinks his name is. We just give him a name that fits and people will use it." Mary repositioned the baby so she could better see his face. "Isn't that right, William?" It was more than that new babies are wrinkly and look like old people. There was something here that was connected to something before.

Jules recounted the money, straightened the pile of bills until all of the edges were even, turned the pile on edge and tapped it against the dark wood of the table, turned it and tapped it again, put it down and looked at it, picked it up again and ran his thumb over the edges to make it "thrum", held it under his nose and thrummed it again. He moved the pile to Charlie's glass table and turned the light onto it. It didn't add anything. He turned the light off and looked at the table. "Now what the hell did Charlie want with this thing?" He spoke to the empty hotel room. "If we leave it to Charlie, he'll just waste all that money and nothing good will come of it."

Jules moved the set of keys over, picked up the driver's licence from under them. Looked at the photo. "Robert Muskrat." He looked at it for a long moment. "You know something, Robert, I bet to white people you and I look the same." Jules pocketed the driver's licence, separated the safety deposit box key from the ring and went out to collect the fortune that was surely intended for him.

"Charlie! Charlie!" a man was yelling and nearly running across the lobby of the hotel toward me. "I knew I'd find you here. Everyone from Saskatchewan stays at the Royal York." He was digging through his pockets — left front pants, right front pants, right shirt, left shirt, "I've been checking every hotel in Toronto for days." Lower left suit jacket, lower right suit, outside breast, inside breast, and back to left front pants. He looked up from his body search.

"You don't remember me."

I shook my head. He stopped searching for a moment.

"Trenton."

It didn't bring anything back.

"In a restaurant."

Nothing

"Bert, Bert Russel remember."

I remembered Wesakicak saying something.

"Yeah, and the guy from Indian Affairs showed up and I covered it up so that he couldn't see it. You didn't even finish your steak." Right pants, left pants, right shirt, left shirt, inside breast. "Here it is." Bert held out his hand, opened it to show one of those little white lumpy stones. Then it made sense. Not that I remembered Bert, but that there were forty diamonds. The little man gave me forty diamonds, not thirty-nine. Forty made sense. Forty days and forty nights, forty days in the desert, forty rocks on a fire. Four directions. Four colours. Thirty-nine didn't have any symmetry to it.

"I couldn't keep it. I had to give it back." He took my wrist with his free hand, lifted my hand until it lay flat, and put the diamond in the centre of my palm. I looked up from the stone to the face that smiled, the face of a man pleased with himself, okay with himself.

Over Bert's shoulder, Jules stepped out of an elevator, walked three casual steps toward us, froze for a fraction of a second, then walked quickly toward the door and the street. I wanted to follow him, tell him I was leaving, thank him, but Bert was still holding my wrist.

"So how's your stay been? Toronto's been good to you I hope."

"Toronto's been real good. Brought back lots of memories."

"Good, I'm glad. Man, Charlie, you don't know how glad I am that I found you. That little stone drove me just about nuts. Not just trying to find you, but trying to convince Erica that I had to give it back, that we couldn't keep it."

I looked down at the stone, wondered which memory this might have purchased. Too late. Wesakicak was gone and all I had was a rock, a cold little rock that couldn't hug me or kiss me. I would have given it to Bert, put it back in his hand, and said, 'Thanks, but you can keep it." But one look at his proud face, the face that showed a man who had overcome a huge obstacle and I couldn't take his accomplishment away from him. I put the stone in my shirt pocket, made a mental note of which pocket. Mary might like this. Something about women and diamonds, or maybe that was only a popular myth. I would give it to Mary anyway.

"So, what makes you think Charlie is FAS?"

Thelma looked up from her novel at her sister still holding the sleeping William, both of them swallowed in the deep chair pulled up to the fireplace.

"The other day you said Charlie was FAS. I've been wondering what makes you think that."

Thelma marked her page with a strip of leather and closed the heavy book, rested it on her lap. "Well, he has all the classic symptoms: poor memory, irresponsible, doesn't seem to be able to connect actions with consequences. You know . . . " she stalled.

"No, I don't know."

"It just fits, that's all."

"Maybe because he's Indian."

"Come on, Mary, I'm Indian too."

"Doesn't mean you can't have racist ideas."

"It just fits. I don't have anything against Charlie. He's a nice guy. Maybe I'm wrong about the FAS stuff, who knows. Charlie's different. It was a logical explanation, that's all."

Mary looked down at the sleeping baby. "When Charlie gets home things are going to be different. We're going into a new age."

"The age of grandparents."

"Yeah, the age of grandparents." Mary moved the blanket gently away so that she could better see William's sleeping face.

Not much happened on the drive home from Toronto. Thunder purred, and rode smooth. It was like he knew I had a glass table on the seat beside me and he was being careful. Just before I got home, a few miles North of Timber Bay a Moose walked out onto the highway. Thunder eased to a stop. The rifle slid out easily from behind the seat as the Moose walked slowly back into the trees, looking once over its shoulder to see if I was following. I was.

Carefully, around a stand of Willow, have to be careful of Willow. It will make loud scratchy sounds if it touches you. The Moose was moving through the mix of Pine and Poplar, from my right at an angle across, in front of me. I stopped and listened to him crunch through the remainder of spring snow. A clearing lay open and I knelt on its edge, held my breath, waited. The Moose stopped. We both waited. I checked my shirt pocket for the little good-luck stone. It was there. Then he stepped into the clearing, one, two steps, stop. He turned and looked toward me, and the rifle kicked into my shoulder.

It was late in the day when I pulled Thunder up to the cabin. His gas gauge lay on empty, and when I turned off the key I'm sure I heard him sigh as his engine eased to stillness.

I don't know what Mary did with the diamond I gave her. She kissed me on the cheek. "You're so sweet, Charlie," put it in her pocket, and I never ever saw it again.

The next month was a wonderful time of awakening. Not just that it was spring and I was home and I had a grandson. Every morning I went for a walk just as the sun was beginning a new day. Somewhere down by the shore, looking out over the water, or maybe in the Pines, where they spread apart with lots of space between, or maybe on the edge of the muskeg, where Grandma's trail, the one she used for snaring rabbits, wound through the Spruce and Tamarack, I would pull out the little leather bag, randomly select a bubble and pop it to see what it brought. Most of the memories were things of beauty, things that hurt my heart, stretched it until it ached. Others, were sad. The morning I remembered Grandma's funeral, I returned to the cabin and cried. Mary held me through the sobs, just held me and never said anything.

I found the memory of when I first told Mary I loved her. She would never get me with that again. I remembered it clearly, the pouring rain, the green raincoat we shared, held over our heads, the smell of water turning to steam on hot asphalt, and I thought I needed to give her something to lift her spirits. But I didn't. Her spirit was strong.

Each day I returned home and shared my new memories with her. She listened, and laughed or cried with me. The morning when I remembered the first time we made love, I asked her to marry me, if it wasn't too late.

"Too late? Too late? Charlie Muskrat, I've been waiting thirty years for you to ask."

It felt sort of like we were in a romance novel when she threw her arms around me and peppered my face with tiny kisses.

CHARLIE LET HIS LAST BREATH GO. Let his heart give one final strong drumbeat in the song of his life. He saw the light and walked steadily toward it. Two helpers came and held him by each shoulder, helped him as he floated up above the Earth, through a wall of fire and across the long gap to where Grandma and Grandpa waited for him.

Charlie and Mary lived a long time. They created many good memories together and Charlie kept them, cherished them the way he cherished Mary. Charlie lived to teach William's daughter how to hunt Moose from a canoe, how to call it out of the trees to the river's edge. That was what he was doing the last time he saw a sunrise. He sat in a canoe with the water easy on his paddle as he silently guided it along the shore to give his great-granddaughter a clear shot at the Moose. That night he went to bed tired, and sometime during the night he left.

He looked at the helper on his left, recognized him. "Jules. Oh, it's so good to have a friend here."

"I'm glad you still think of me that way."

"Always." Charlie turned to see who was holding his right shoulder. The face smiled, introduced itself. "Wesley Jack."

"You don't fool me this time, Wesakicak." Charlie laughed, then thought about it. The Trickster was coming to take him. "What direction are you taking me?" he asked, suddenly serious.

Wesakicak laughed so hard they all had to stop, in a huddle, three men with their arms around each other's shoulders. "You are such a comedian, Charlie."

Born and raised in Northern Saskatchewan, HAROLD JOHNSON has a Master of Law degree from Harvard University. He has served in the Canadian Navy, and worked in mining and logging. Johnson is the author of two novels, *Billy Tinker* (Thistledown Press) and *Back Track* (Thistledown Press), both shortlisted for Saskatchewan Book Awards. *Back Track* was also shortlisted for Aboriginal Book of the Year and Fiction Book of the Year, Anskohk Book Awards. His most recent publication *Two Families: Treaties and Government* (Purich Publishing) won a 2007 Saskatchewan Book Award.

Johnson practices law in La Ronge, Saskatchewan, and balances this with operating his family's traditional trap line using a dog team.